Inspector Sinclair and Sergeant Powers' most interesting cases

Ray Filby

==

Inspector Sinclair and Sergeant Powers' most Interesting cases

Publisher : Midhurst

Published by Midhurst

Copyright © Ray Filby 2019

This is a work of fiction.
Any resemblance to actual persons,
living or dead, is purely coincidental.

Midhurst.
2, Freers Mews,
Warwick,
Warwickshire,
CV34 6DP

ISBN 978-1-9996835-0-4

http://midhurstpublishing.uk

Acknowledgements

The author would like to thank his wife, Sue, both for proof reading and for her patience and encouragement during the writing of these stories.

Contents

<u>Introduction</u>

Unlike the traditional 'Whodunnit', the stories in this volume do not leave the reader guessing until the end when the detective discloses clues which only he or she had identified as significant and which enable him or her to solve a case which has had everyone else baffled.

The scenarios which lead to an unexplained death are described under the subheading, **'the Event'**. Before reading further, you, the reader, may wish to speculate on the means by which the death was effected and by whom but in the absence of evidence, this will be no more than guesswork..

The section following the event is sub-headed, **'the Investigation'** and describes the systematic way the detectives set about unravelling the mystery. You, the reader, are kept informed of each step of the investigation and as you weigh each piece of evidence as it comes to light, you may even be ahead of the detectives in working out how the murder was committed and by whom.

A final subsection headed **'the Evidence'** is included in each story which summarises the significance of the evidence which has been unearthed during the investigation and the conclusions which could be drawn from it.

I often find when reading detective stories, that if there are many individuals involved, I can quickly lose track of which character is which. I have therefore included at the beginning of each story a list of the main characters to which the reader can refer back, should the identity or role of any particular character be forgotten as the story unfolds.

Chapter 1

<u>An unexplained car accident</u>

Victim - Eleanor Weston – had apparently run her
car over the cliff near Beachy Head.

Cornelius Weston – Eleanor's husband
James Weston   – Cornelius and Eleanor's son
Josephine Barton – James' girlfriend
Elizabeth Wise   – living opposite Cornelius
                                     and Eleanor.
Joan Richards   – Cornelius' secret girlfriend.
Harriette Henderson - friend of Eleanor.
Kevin and Sheila
        Graham   – the Weston's neighbours

<u>The Event</u>

Earlswith was a seaside resort, not too far from
Eastbourne. Whereas Eastbourne had survived
the post-war boom when it was the norm to for
families to take seaside holidays, and it was still
a prosperous, even prestigious, south coast resort,
Earlswith was distinctly rundown. Many of the
once splendid hotels which lined the esplanade
were now deserted shells. The peeling paintwork
of the hotels which remained in business clearly

spoke that fresh rendering and decorating was needed to restore them to the glory they had enjoyed in their Edwardian heyday.

Eleanor Weston had lived in Earlswith since marrying Cornelius nearly thirty years earlier. Her rather dowdy appearance concealed a woman with a warm heart and pleasant personality. Eleanor's clothing could be described as definitely retro, but at least, her scuffed flat brown shoes co-ordinated with the muddy colours she usually wore.

Although normally calm and placid, a number of things were happening in Eleanor's life which left her feeling tense and uneasy. For the most part, Eleanor was easy going and non-confrontational, but recently she had cause to complain to the Grahams, her neighbours, about a series of raucous parties they had held which had continued into the small hours. The noise had deprived the Westons of sleep. Although she had approached Sheila Graham in a measured and calm manner about the problem, she was met with a torrent of abuse and accused of being a busybody and killjoy.

"Why don't you go and throw yourself off a cliff?"

was Sheila's final and unjustified unkind retort. What had upset Eleanor most was not this uncalled for abuse but the refusal of Cornelius to give her any support in this matter.

Eleanor was a sensitive soul and for a day or so, this bitter altercation weighed on her mind, causing her to become absentminded. To her embarrassment, when she went shopping the following day, as she distractedly put a jar of washing detergent in her basket without it first having been properly scanned, the electronic voice in the supermarket self-service area had announced,

'There is an unexpected item in your basket!'

Inquisitive eyes turned on her as the member of supermarket staff superintending this area came to investigate the problem.

Eleanor was experiencing further anxiety over her sense that Cornelius was being unnecessarily secretive. He would come home late, explaining his lateness with what Eleanor perceived to be obvious lies. If Eleanor unexpectedly came into a room where it was clear that he had been making a phone call, he would quickly turn off his mobile phone without completing the call.

A further cause for Eleanor's anxiety lay in her son, James', intention to set up home with his girlfriend, Josephine (Jo), while still an undergraduate at Leeds University. He had asked his parents for a significant sum of money to put down as a deposit on a house. Cornelius and Eleanor thought that James should complete his degree first before setting up home with his partner. Not only did they not particularly like James' girlfriend, Jo, but they were disappointed by the fact that they intended to live together rather than get married first. James was the sole beneficiary of his parents' wills and most of the family's capital was in Eleanor's name as she had been a relatively wealthy woman when she married Cornelius.

Then tragedy struck. Cornelius was looking smart. He usually did. He had put on a suit for his recent visit to Earlswith library. The doorbell rang and he answered the door to a pair of police constables, PC George Alexander and WPC Helen Smith. They looked grave and asked if they could come in. Cornelius showed them to his front room, anxiously waiting for what news they might be bringing him. Helen Smith spoke first and asked Cornelius to prepare himself for a shock. A car had been driven over the cliff near Beachy Head and the only occupant was identified as Eleanor. It would appear that this event had occurred about one hour earlier but no-one had actually witnessed the accident apart from the occupants of a fishing vessel some way out to sea who had alerted the coastguard via their radio link.

Cornelius was normally a serious man but now he looked graver than usual, no, he looked aghast. He put his head in his hands and sat there for some moments before resuming his posture.

"Had you any reason for suspecting your wife might be preparing to take her own life?" asked PC George Alexander.

"Not at all," replied Cornelius, quite visibly shaken by the news. "I know that she was a bit depressed recently but not to the extent that she would commit suicide."

The constables expressed their sympathy and told Cornelius that they would be in touch when the inquest on this tragic death was convened. Cornelius declined the offer that they might find someone to spend time with him while he came to terms with this news. They said goodbye to a clearly shocked Cornelius on the doorstep as they left. Cornelius immediately phoned his son, James, to inform him of the tragedy which had just occurred.

Further investigation by the police uncovered evidence that this was not a suicide but murder, leaving the inevitable question to be answered, 'Who dunnit?'

It shouldn't be difficult for you, the reader, to decide on the guilty party fairly early as you read about the following investigation. How it was done may be more difficult to fathom out.

The Investigation

The officers called upon to investigate this crime were Detective Inspector Peter Sinclair and his assistant, Detective Sergeant Christine (Chris) Powers. Peter and Chris had first worked together when she had been given a special dispensation to go to Grimthorpe to assist in the investigation of the murder of Chris's sister, Joan. It was thought that Chris might have special family knowledge which could have bearing on that case. Peter and Chris quickly realised that they hit it off well and managed to arrange that they should be partnered as investigating officers. The fact that they were both prominent members of their local Anglican churches helped to cement the partnership.

Peter Sinclair was a clean shaven, tall upright man in his early fifties. When on duty, he was usually found to be smartly dressed in a tailored, charcoal grey, Moss Bros suit. His shoes were always well cleaned but not with a parade ground polish. Peter's slightly grey hair was neatly parted on the left and he wore rimless glasses.

Chris was also very smartly dressed, usually in a navy skirt suit from Next, but she had similar bottle green and chocolate brown suits which she frequently wore as an alternative to her preferred navy. She was about 5ft 6 ins tall, stockily built but certainly not fat. When on duty, she wore smart but comfortable black shoes and she walked with a confident manner which might have given the impression that she had formerly been in the services.

Their superintendent briefed them on the findings of the Scene of Crime Officers (SOCOS). The driver, Eleanor, was not wearing a seat belt but the fall over the cliff had not been the cause of death. The police pathologist ascertained that Eleanor had been strangled and this had taken place some twenty-four hours before the plunge of the car over the cliff edge. It appeared that the engine had probably been running at the time the car went over, but the gear was in neutral, clear evidence that the car had been pushed. The steering wheel had been wiped clear of prints. Because it was raining at the time of the incident, there was little evidence of what had happened to be found at the top of the cliff from where the car had been pushed. There were clear tyre marks but any footprints had been obscured as a result of the persistent rain.

Peter and Chris went to examine the wrecked car but there was nothing they could find which was any more relevant than had already been ascertained by the SOCOS. Similarly, they could discover no more evidence as they walked along the cliff edge where the car had been pushed over. Neither was there anything they could learn from Eleanor's body which hadn't already been discovered by the pathologist. They had a look at Eleanor's clothing. Her brown outer garments were still wet from the rain which had been falling on the day of the murder.

The first port of call for Peter and Chris was the home of Cornelius and Eleanor. Cornelius opened the door and ushered them in to the front room where a shocked James was waiting, having immediately returned home from Leeds on hearing his father's news. The room was tidy with pleasant wallpaper, tasteful ornaments and a vase of artificial flowers. It showed signs of a loving feminine touch. After expressing the usual pleasantries and condolences, they broke the news that Eleanor's death was now the subject of a murder investigation. Cornelius and James looked shocked. Whoever would have wanted to murder Eleanor? She was a lovely woman without an enemy in the world.

Peter started the questioning, explaining that in a case like this, initially, everyone with any connection to Eleanor was a suspect. As apparently the last person to see Eleanor alive, Peter asked Cornelius if he could account for his actions from the time that Eleanor left home.

Cornelius started. "I had just gone across the road to ask Elizabeth if she would look out for the postman as it was possible that a package was going to be delivered which might be too large to pass through the letter box. Eleanor waved to us as she drove off. This was about 9 o'clock on Wednesday. It was lightly raining and she switched on the windscreen wipers as she turned to go down the road. I believe that she was going to visit her friend, Harriet Henderson, who lives in Eastbourne. About five minutes later, I went to the library, returned the books I had borrowed and asked the assistant if she could direct me to the Egyptology section. Ancient Egypt has always had a particular fascination for me and I am widely read on the subject. I spent about an hour and a half, browsing through the books and then checked out a particular volume I wanted to study at home."

Cornelius pointed to the book on the coffee table, Geddes and Grosses's 'Ancient Egypt, Myth and History'

"I was beginning to get worried that Eleanor hadn't returned when two police officers called with the shocking news. But what is it that makes you think this was murder?"

"We are not at liberty to disclose that at present but it will all be explained at the inquest. Did anybody see you during the time you were reading in the library?"

"Yes of course. The library was quite crowded but there was no-one I recognised as being personally known to myself to confirm my story. However, there should be timestamps registered on the books I returned and loaned out. At times like this, one is glad that the computers which have become part of modern life can back up our stories. I'm sure the librarian will remember speaking to me."

Chris now took up the questioning and spoke to James.

"I'm sorry we need to talk to you in depth so soon after the loss of your mother. As my colleague explained, at this stage of the investigation, we have to regard everyone as suspects. Can you recount for your movements on Wednesday, 7th November?"

"That's no problem. In the morning I attended lectures. When Dad phoned, I was having lunch with my university friends in Leeds. I can give you the names of at least five of my friends who can verify that."

Peter now had a question for Cornelius.

"Did your wife have any trouble with the neighbours?"

"We normally get on well with the neighbours but there was an altercation a week ago when Eleanor complained about the noise being made at a late night party."

"Well, thank you. I think that covers everything for the time being. We'll now go and have a chat with your neighbours and the lady who lives opposite. Can you remind us of their names?"

"Our neighbours are Kevin and Sheila Graham and the lady opposite is Elizabeth Wise."

"One other thing. Could you let us have your phone numbers, mobile and landline, in case we need to make urgent contact with you? We'll need to speak with Harriet Henderson. Can you give us her address?"

After Cornelius and James had provided the information requested, Peter and Chris thanked them for their help and made their way next door. Sheila Graham answered the door, wiping her hands on the fairly grubby apron she was wearing. Peter announced who they were, showing his warrant card, and asked if they could ask a few questions. On being shown into a somewhat untidy reception room, Sheila had to clear piles of papers from chairs to enable them to get seated, Peter and Chris took in the environment. The windows needed cleaning and there was a perceptible layer of dust on the chimney piece. The carpet needed hoovering too.

Peter explained why they had come.

Sheila was aghast.

"I wondered what the police car activity was next-door but I find it hard to believe that Eleanor has been murdered."

Peter outlined what had happened, giving only the necessary detail, and asked if Sheila could account for her whereabouts on Wednesday morning.

"You surely can't think that I had anything to do with Eleanor's death," said Sheila, blanching at the thought she might be a murder suspect.

"This is routine," explained Peter. "Everyone with any connection with Eleanor is a suspect at this stage."

Sheila recounted her movements. She explained that she had been shopping all Wednesday morning and gave the names of three friends she had met at different times during the morning who could vouch for her alibi.

"I feel absolutely dreadful now," she said. "Eleanor and I had a bit of a barney a week or so back and I told her to go and jump off a cliff. In a way, considering how badly chosen my words were, I'm glad to discover she was murdered rather that committing suicide in this dreadful way. But of course, I hate to think that a neighbour has been murdered. We normally got on well but I'd had a bit too much to drink that morning and I'm now ashamed I spoke in the way I did. There was no call for it.".

"Can you tell us where your husband was?"

"Yes. He was at work at Starling Tools where he's a machinist. I'm sure you will find his work colleagues will bear out that he didn't skip work that day."

After thanking Sheila, Peter and Chris made their way over to Elizabeth's house and went through the normal formalities before being admitted into the reception room. How different rooms can be in neighbours' houses of identical design.

Elizabeth's reception room was smart as a new pin with tasteful ornaments on the chimney piece and a bunch of alstromerias in a vase on the coffee table. Peter and Chris declined the offer of tea or coffee.

Like Sheila, Elizabeth had wondered what the police activity had been at the Weston's house and was similarly shocked at what had happened to a lady she liked and knew well. Elizabeth explained her activities on the day in question.

"Cornelius came over at about nine o'clock to ask me to look out for the postman as he was expecting delivery of a parcel. Eleanor drove out while we were speaking."

"Are you sure it was Eleanor driving?" asked Chris.

"Well, yes. She waved to us as she drove out. Who else could it have been?"

"Did you notice anything unusual about her?" Chris continued.

Elizabeth thought for a while.

"Yes, she was wearing dark glasses which was a bit unusual on a drab November morning. She was also wearing a bright yellow raincoat which she normally only wears at weekends, but of course, this seemed the right thing to be wearing as it was raining. I didn't get a very clear view of her face as she'd only just started the car. Water was streaming down the windscreen and she didn't turn on the windscreen wipers until she was turning out of the drive."

Elizabeth hadn't left the house that morning but had made several phone calls to friends and relations.

"What did you make of all that?" Peter asked Chris as they left Elizabeth's house.

"This is going to be a fairly easy case to solve," she said. "We know that Eleanor was killed the day before that Wednesday so Cornelius was obviously lying. His is the only weak alibi among those to whom we spoke. He would have had plenty of time between booking into the library and booking out again to dispose of the car over the cliff. The cliffs near Beachy Head are less than a quarter of an hour's drive from Earlswith

Library. In a crowded and busy library, it's unlikely that even the librarian would have noticed him surreptitiously leaving and returning. Also, the woman seen leaving the Weston house that morning was differently dressed from the woman recovered from the car. Clearly, a woman is involved as an accomplice to Cornelius!"

"I agree," said Peter. "When a suspect provides superfluous information to verify an alibi like pointing us to the timestamps of the library booking in and out system, and making a point of being noticed by the librarian at the beginning and end of the time he claims he stayed in the library, one's suspicions are immediately aroused. However, we can't make an arrest yet until we can identify the woman involved. This may take a week or so. Cornelius will suspect that we will the monitoring his communications and will have arranged not to make contact with this woman for maybe two or three weeks by which time he will probably assume that he's no longer being observed. So, it's a case of *cherchez la femme.* I think that as this is a murder inquiry, the Chief Constable will authorise the monitoring of suspects' phones."

"What next?" asked Chris.

"I think a word with Eleanor's friend, Harriet Henderson might be useful."

Peter and Chris found Harriet not unsurprisingly shocked by the news of her friend's violent death. No, Eleanor hadn't arranged to call on her that Wednesday morning. When asked if she was aware of any worries Eleanor might have been experiencing, they were not surprised to discover that Eleanor had confided in her that Cornelius' behaviour was causing concern. His unexplained late homecomings and his suddenly terminating phone conversations when she unexpectedly entered a room where he was on the phone, had led her to believe that Cornelius was seeing another woman.

As they left Harriet's house, Peter suggested that they should examine the traffic surveillance camera's footage for that fateful Wednesday. A lot could be learned if they could track the movement of the Weston's car through Earlswith and Eastbourne.

"In spite of Cornelius' boast that modern computer systems would confirm his alibi, he may well find that surveillance camera footage would seal his downfall." Peter stated.

The surveillance camera information was indeed useful. The Weston's blue Toyota could be seen entering Earlswith and leaving the town on the camera at the other end of town. However, while it should have taken no more than three or four minutes to drive through Earlswith as it was not a big or congested town, the surveillance cameras indicated a delay of twenty minutes between the car's appearances on the two cameras. They were unable to get a clear view of the driver. The Eastbourne cameras showed the car passing through Eastbourne at a predictable rate. It was also noticed that the Toyota was being followed by a black Fiat as it left Earlswith and it was still there as the Toyota passed through Eastbourne. The car number plates could be made out on both cars from the Eastbourne cameras. The black Fiat was seen returning through Eastbourne and Earlswith twenty minutes later. The black Fiat's owner was traced as a Mrs Joan Richards.

Meanwhile, the Weston's phone records were carefully scrutinised. The names of several women who had received calls were identified. These could have been friends of either Cornelius or Eleanor, but when Joan Richards was shown to have been the recipient of a number of calls, Peter and Chris knew that they had found the suspect woman.

They called round to Joan's house armed with a search warrant. The door was opened by Joan, a slim, very attractive woman wearing a green house-coat, grey track suit bottom and white trainers. She was probably in her mid-thirties. She had shoulder length blond hair and china blue eyes. Joan would not have looked out of place as a presenter on a glamour show like 'Strictly Come Dancing' or as a judge on 'Britain's got Talent'. Peter and Chris independently wondered why such an apparently lovely woman should have become associated with someone like Cornelius, especially to the extent of doing something which was going to get her into serious trouble. However, they could see that the prospect of establishing a long-term relationship with this glamourous woman would certainly be a motive for Cornelius deciding to murder his wife!

Joan expressed surprise that they should have called on her in connection with the murder of a woman she didn't know. Joan claimed that she believed she had been at a Yoga class on the Wednesday in question. She made no objection to their searching the house without their need to produce the search warrant, unaware that there was incriminating evidence in her home. Peter and Chris found what they were looking for in the wardrobe in an upstairs bedroom, a yellow raincoat with a tab bearing Eleanor Weston's name. Joan persisted in claiming she didn't know Eleanor. This was probably true. She said that Cornelius had lent her the raincoat when it started to rain when they had met one evening at a restaurant. She wasn't able to account for why Cornelius would have brought his wife's coat to the restaurant anyway.

Cornelius was arrested on a charge of murdering has wife and Joan as his accomplice. Meanwhile, Peter and Chris worked out the details of how the crime must have been committed.

The Evidence

The state of Eleanor's body.
Cornelius was very naïve if he thought that the police would just accept what appeared on face value of his wife meeting her death as a result of driving over a cliff. The fact that the pathologist's investigation revealed that Eleanor had been strangled immediately indicated that a murder had been committed. Had Cornelius bludgeoned his wife to death, her injuries may have seemed more consistent with having been sustained while the car was driven over the cliff but the pathologist would have discovered from the state of the body that death had occurred at least as early as the previous day.

The car seen by Elizabeth Wise, driven off from their house by Eleanor.
While Peter and Chris immediately realised that Cornelius was the murderer, he clearly had a female accomplice. Premature arrest of Cornelius would have driven this accomplice underground and made it difficult for the police to trace her. The driver had taken steps to prevent Elizabeth getting a really clear view of her face. She was wearing dark glasses when leaving the house as

Cornelius was speaking to Elizabeth. She waved to Cornelius and Elizabeth but didn't turn on the windscreen wipers until she had turned out of the drive. Elizabeth would have had no reason at the time to suspect that the driver was anyone but Eleanor. The fact that Joan was wearing different clothing from the clothes in which the body Eleanor was discovered, was a pointer to another piece of important evidence. It was more than likely that the yellow coat was still at the home of Cornelius's accomplice and this indeed turned out to be the case, providing damning evidence against Joan.

Peter and Chris had been surprised that a glamourous woman like Joan should have been closely associated with an older and fairly ordinary man like Cornelius. However, Joan had just come through a messy divorce and this was probably a rebound relationship. In her past, Joan had run two failing businesses, which suggested that Joan was a risk taker.

Information provided by the traffic surveillance cameras.
The delay between the Toyota, supposedly being driven by Eleanor entering and leaving Earlswith

was an indication that the car was delayed to enable another part of the plot to be enacted. This gave time for Cornelius to walk the short distance to the library, get his books time-stamped and draw the librarian's attention to himself. Getting the books he borrowed time-stamped and drawing the librarian's attention to himself as he left the library later did not provide Cornelius with what he believed to be a cast iron alibi. He had plenty of time to continue with his crime, just taking care that he left the library unobtrusively and returned later without being noticed. Cornelius's drawing Peter and Chris's attention to the evidence of the times when he entered and left the library led them to suspect that this was a set up alibi.

When the traffic surveillance cameras again picked up Cornelius's Toyota, it was being followed by a Fiat. The fact that these cars were again seen in convoy by the Eastbourne traffic surveillance cameras led the detectives to suspect that this was the second car involved in the crime which would be needed for Cornelius to return to Earlswith in time. It was indeed seen entering the town at a time which would be expected if dropping off Cornelius by the library was the plan. It was a mistake on Cornelius and Joan's part to drive the cars in convoy so that they could be associated. Had the Fiat left some time before or after the Toyota among other traffic, it's unlikely the association would have been made and it would have taken the police much longer to trace Cornelius's accomplice. The Fiat number plate picked up by the surveillance cameras made it easy to trace Joan and the fact that her name appeared among phone calls made from the Weston's phones confirmed that she was the accomplice. Eventually, Cornelius would have contacted Joan and she would have come under police surveillance but by then she would have probably disposed of Eleanor's coat.

The setting of the car's gear
The car was in neutral, even though it appeared that the engine might have been running during the plunge over the cliff.

This points to the fact that it was almost certain that the car was pushed over the cliff after Eleanor had been manoeuvred into position. It would not have been easy, even with two of them, to transfer Eleanor's body from where it must have been hidden under a blanket on the back seat into the driving position. They were lucky that there were no dog walkers around or anybody else to observe what was going on on this remote stretch of cliff head. The occupant of the boat which observed the car plunge was too far out to see what had caused the plunge. He would not have been focused to expect such an event anyway.

"The couple really underestimated how thorough the police would be in investigating an apparent suicide," said Peter as they talked about the case later. "I think they thought that the police would assume that Eleanor had been killed as the car plunged over the cliff, not recognising that the pathologist would be able to ascertain the actual cause and approximate time of death."

Chapter 2

The Mossdale Orchestra

Victim - James Cummings - Cornet player

Members of Mossdale Orchestra

Sir Joseph Canning	- Director
Arthur Northfield	- Conductor
Gordon Bains	- Trombonist
Inderjit Singh	- 1st Violinist
Harry Cartwright	- Percussionist
Ahmed Khan	- Oboist
Miriam Oldroyd	- Flautist
Mrs. Joan Edwards	-James' landlady

The Event

The coach pulled up outside the Black Bear, Mossdale's most popular hostelry where the popular brand of beer was always perfectly cooled and served by Mary and Frank Rhodes, the charming and genial landlords. The members of Mossdale Orchestra were in a jovial mood as they left the coach, having spent a successful weekend performing at the seaside resort of Shepherdsford.

They trooped into the pub for a final celebratory drink, leaving the coach driver to unload their instruments and cases from the hold. The cases were all identical, but identifiable by the owner's label and pairs of coloured ribbon tied round the handles.

In the past, when the members had cases of varying size and shape, problems had arisen in loading the hold and getting on the instruments as well. By their nature, the instrument cases could not be standardised but by having all the suitcases of a moderate size and the same shape, it was possible to get everything into the hold of the Mercury Travel Co. coach. This firm was local, efficient and inexpensive and an obvious choice to transport the members of the orchestra when performing away from Mossdale. The standardisation of case sizes was an arrangement which had been put in place by the orchestra's director, Sir Joseph Canning, who also had the idea of using coloured ribbons to enable the cases to be more quickly and easily identified than by scrutinizing the labels. Having worked in electronics, it was natural for Sir Joseph to hit upon the idea of using the resistance colour coding system as a means of associating a number with each case.

Black	0	Orange	3	Blue	6
Brown	1	Yellow	4	Violet	7
Red	2	Green	5	Grey	8
				White	9

The members of the orchestra had all been allocated identification numbers between 1 and 100. The first digit of their number was represented by the ribbon tied next to the traditional name label. Thus an orange ribbon next to the name label, accompanied by a green ribbon was No. 35. This was the identification number of Harry Cartwright, the percussionist. Arthur Northfield, the conductor, had a black followed by a brown ribbon which represented 01.

After about forty minutes, the members of the orchestra started to leave the Black Bear, retrieve their cases and make their separate ways home. The last to leave for home were Arthur Northfield and Miriam Oldroyd. Miriam was tee total and was always public spirited enough to mount guard over the cases in the pub car park until the drinking session was over.

The orchestra wasn't a completely happy bunch. The fly in the ointment was the cornet player, James Cummings. James was middle aged, slovenly dressed and had bad breath. He did manage to scrub up to a satisfactory standard when he donned a dinner jacket to fulfil his role, seated among the rest of the orchestra. James had absolutely no sense of acceptable social behaviour. He was loud mouthed. He made distasteful remarks about other members of the orchestra and then guffawed loudly as if he had said something funny. He was oblivious to the antagonism he was creating within the orchestra. Surprisingly, for such an insensitive person, James was an absolutely divine instrumentalist and his cornet solo was often the high point of a performance by Mossdale orchestra.

Ahmed Khan, the oboist, was one of the main targets for James' misplaced humour. Ahmed was sensitive about being banded as a member of the same religious group as the Islamic extremists who were responsible for so many atrocities around the world. By contrast, Ahmed was a very quiet, peace-loving man and he felt extremely insulted on the occasions when James came out with a stream of anti-Islamic jokes.

The person in the orchestra who loathed James the most was the flautist, Miriam Oldroyd. Her daughter had been run over and seriously injured by a car driven by James. The inquest had absolved James of any blame. Miriam's daughter had been observed to just step out in front of James' car without looking up and down the road. However, this event had left Miriam antagonistic towards James and this was made more acute when James referred to her as 'Jaywalker Mum'.

James referred to other members of the orchestra by nicknames he had made up. Harry Cartwright, the percussionist, was referred to as 'Mr. Bumpetty Bump Bump Bump'. Inderjit Singh, the leader of the orchestra, was referred as 'Tallboy Turbanhead'. The nickname he used to the conductor, Arthur Northfield's, face was 'King Arthur' which sounded reasonable but when out of earshot, King Arthur was corrupted to 'King 'alf a brain missing'.

James left the pub with the rest of the band, picked up his case and returned home. His landlady was out so he made his way to his room to unpack and wait for Mrs. Edwards return when he knew she would make him a cup of tea. Half an hour later, Mrs. Edwards returned. Joan

Edwards was a stout, homely woman who tended to mother her lodgers. She had long learned to cope with James' rudeness and misplaced sense of humour. James coat was hanging in the hall so she knew he was home. She called out to him and put on the kettle to make tea. When James didn't answer or come down, Joan knocked on his door. Still no answer. She cautiously opened the door. What a shock! James was lying unconscious on the floor, his open case resting on the bed, but there was an even greater shock! Coiled on the floor next to James was a lurid green snake!

Joan slammed the door shut and immediately phoned the emergency services, police and ambulance, and informed them of the situation, warning them that there was an almost certainly venomous snake in James' room and specialist help might be needed to deal with it.

The emergency services arrived within seven minutes but to conform to standing orders, they had to wait outside James' room for the arrival of a person who was competent to handle venomous snakes. The nearest zoo was about thirty miles away and it was almost an hour later when a member of the zoo staff arrived. He dressed himself in protective clothing which included specialist gloves and a helmet with a transparent visor in case this snake turned out to be of the spitting variety. He cautiously entered the room with his snake handling stick and carrying box. Within five minutes he was out again with the snake secure in the carrying box. He announced that the snake was the extremely venomous green mamba. As it appeared that it had bitten James, he was now, almost certainly dead. He assured them that the body was quite safe to handle. James' body was then strapped on to a stretcher and transported to hospital where the fatality was confirmed.

You, the reader, are invited to ponder how and why had this crime been carried out.

The Investigation

Detective Inspector Peter Sinclair and his assistant, Detective Sergeant Christine (Chris) Powers were given the responsibility of investigating the case.

"An obvious question which needs to be answered," ventured Chris, "is however did the snake get into James' case?"

"I don't think the snake got into James' case," said Peter. "I think that James' case must have been swapped with a case containing the snake. Let's examine the case."

They were met in the forensic laboratory by Dr. Edward Cooper. The case in question had been modified. A few unobtrusive air holes had been drilled in it. It contained the remains of what appeared to be small rodents which must have been put there as food for the snake. Taped to the sides of the case away from the ventilation holes were a few small damp pillows which would provide moisture for the snake as well as protecting the snake from being buffeted as the case was moved, and would also provide the weight which matched it to a case containing clothing.

Dr. Cooper explained that it was impossible to tell how long the snake had been boxed up but it was probably unnecessary to have provided food. Being reptiles, snakes can survive long periods without food or water.

They went to see the body.

"Yes," Dr. Cooper confirmed, "The pathologist's report stated that there is no doubt that the victim died from the effect of the snake's venom."

Peter and Chris's next port of call was James' digs. Joan Edwards welcomed them in. Our detectives assessed her as a bustling and perhaps fussy but well-meaning and warm woman.

"What a terrible thing to happen. However did that snake get into James' belongings? If I hadn't been quick and shut the door as soon as I saw that horrible creature, I could well have suffered the same fate as James," she shuddered.

They looked round James' room which the police had told Mrs. Edwards to leave untouched for the time being. The room was sparse and surprisingly tidy. The single bed was made up with an ornately covered duvet. A few novels stood between bookends on the desk which were made to appear that the books were held in position by models of a man and a woman pushing from opposite ends. James' clothes were stored a Stag Minstrel mahogany wardrobe and a matching set of drawers. They looked carefully through the drawers and into the wardrobe but there was nothing in them of any significance. Peter and Chris then went out to have a further chat with Joan Edwards.

"I won't say he didn't have problems," began Joan, "but he was a good tenant. Although he wasn't a smart dresser, his room was always tidy and he was punctual. Sometimes I got a bit fed up with him playing his trumpet thing but as I'm a bit deaf, that didn't worry me very much. He was very amusing though. He used to call the members of the orchestra by funny names. He used to call the conductor 'King 'alf a' brain missing'. The drummer was called 'Mr. Bumpetty Bump Bump Bump'. He pretended that one member of the orchestra was a militant Islamic extremist. A person I think you should visit is a Sikh gentleman whom James referred to as 'Mr. Turban Top'. James claimed that 'Mr. Turban Top's' house was a refuge for illegal immigrants. No one would check up on the house because it was full of poisonous snakes, man eating lizards, crocodiles and alligators. Perhaps that's where the snake came from."

"Did James mention anyone in the orchestra with whom he didn't get on well?" asked Chris.

"I think he had his arguments with most of them," replied Joan, "but the one he seemed most concerned over was one he called 'Jaywalker Mum'. It seems she was always very nasty to him after he hit her daughter in a car accident, but it wasn't James' fault. During the court hearing, it was reported that the girl stepped out right in front of the car, and although he wasn't going fast, James couldn't stop in time."

Chris had recorded most of this in her notebook.

"Well, thank you, Mrs. Edwards," said Peter. "That's been very helpful. We may need to call in again if any further important details need clearing up.”

“What did you make of that?” Peter asked Chris as they left the house.

“We certainly need to pay Inderjit Singh a visit,” said Chris “and as we looked through the wardrobe, it struck me that there was something else we needed to be looking for.”

“James’ dinner jacket which he would have worn during a performance,” answered James, complementing Chris’s thought.

The next stage of the investigation was to interview members of the orchestra starting with the conductor, Arthur Northfield.

“Yes. It was a shock for all of us,” Arthur said as he replied to Peter’s first question. “I’m rather ashamed to say that no-one in the orchestra, including myself, seems to be even slightly upset that James is dead, but of course, he was a fellow human being and we should all be concerned that he met such a terrible end. Who’d want to kill James? He really was an obnoxious personality but the members of the orchestra have broad shoulders. Rather than feeling upset at his jibes, they were all rather sympathetic that he should continuously make such an ass of himself. I can't think of anyone who would have felt so offended that they would actually want to murder James."

Arthur then gave examples of the insulting behaviour that James had shown to almost every member of the orchestra, including mentioning the fraught relationship which existed between James and Inderjit Singh, Miriam Oldroyd and Ahmed Khan.

"Then of course," he continued, "there's what we might call professional jealousy, although of course we're all amateur musicians. Whatever his faults, James' musicianship was superb. His solos were the high point of many of our performances. It seems incongruous that such a rude, socially insensitive person could exhibit so much sensitivity as he performed on his cornet. Were it not for this ability, I would have asked him to leave the orchestra long ago. There'll be no great difficulty in filling his post. We have too many trombonists and Gordon Bains will jump at the chance of moving from the trombone section to play the cornet."

Chris asked Arthur if he could suggest how the snake might have got into the country. It's not the sort of creature one would keep as a pet, and surely, a licence is needed if one wants to have custody of such an animal.

"Some of our members have been abroad in recent months, Harry Cartwright to South Africa, Ahmed Khan to Pakistan and Inderjit Singh to India," Arthur explained. "I suppose you can get poisonous snakes in these countries but I think you'd have great difficulty in smuggling them through customs."

Our detectives realised that they would have to continue by systematically interviewing the members of the orchestra. In view of his recent visit to South Africa, they decided to first visit Harry Cartwright, the percussionist.

"Yes, James wasn't a well-liked character," Harry explained, "but he was tolerated because his expertise on the cornet contributed so much to the success of the performances of Mossdale

Orchestra. However, I can't think of anyone who disliked him sufficiently to bump him off. I expect you've come to me because you've heard that I've been to Africa and might possibly have returned with a snake. That's a long shot. You wouldn't be able to smuggle a creature like that through customs. The snake was probably obtained through a purveyor of exotic animals."

The next member of the orchestra they called on was Ahmed Khan. It had been suggested to Peter and Chris that offending a devout Moslem on the basis of his religion could invite a violent response but they knew that this attitude was unfair to the vast majority of peace loving Moslems and Ahmed had been described to them as being of a peaceable nature. The door was answered by Mrs. Fatima Khan in typical Muslim attire for a woman. Her head was covered with a hijab and she wore a floral tunic over white trousers. On her feet were a pair of black sandals. She showed them into a reception room where Ahmed was in the company of a man who it turned out was another member of the orchestra, Gordon Bains, the trombonist. Gordon was dressed in a loose navy jumper and grey slacks. Ahmed was in typical Moslem clothes, a thobe over a white serwal and wearing a bisht as an overgarment.

"We know why you've come round to see us," said Ahmed as they were shown in before Peter could make a formal introduction. "Yes, we should be sorry to lose a colleague but sadly, there wasn't much love lost between James and most of the orchestra. However, I don't think any of us disliked him enough to kill him in such a barbaric manner. Yes, he insulted Mohammed and did other things which a Moslem like myself would find offensive, but I earned the sympathy of my fellow musicians because of his rudeness. I really felt sorry for the poor chap who couldn't avoid making a fool of himself. He never seemed to appreciate this however. He certainly had a thick skin. Anyway, I wasn't the only one James insulted. We were prepared to accept this as the cost of retaining him as one of our star players. I think we got so used to James' rudeness that in the end it was what you might call, 'water off a duck's back'."

When asked if he kept reptiles, Ahmed explained that his children had a pet tortoise and no, he didn't smuggle in a snake from Pakistan. He pointed out that green mambas don't live in Pakistan anyway.

The presence of Gordon in Ahmed's house saved Peter and Chris the trouble of making a separate call and the questioning turned to him. Gordon laughed when Peter told him that they'd heard that Gordon might take over James' position as the orchestra's main cornet player.

"I didn't want the position so badly that I was prepared to kill for it! Indeed, I'm rather apprehensive. For all his faults, James really was the master of the cornet and I'm afraid that unfavourable comparison may be made on our musicianship, the first time I'm called upon to play a solo."

"Nonsense," interjected Ahmed. "James may have been good but he wasn't so much better than you, and if comparisons are going to be made, you'd be favoured over James on almost every score except perhaps over some of the more difficult cornet solo pieces. I've every confidence that you'll soon be up to James' standard and in time, will be even better."

Gordan smiled, appreciating this compliment.

Neither Gordon nor James had any theory as to how the snake got into James bag.

"I'm sure there were other people besides members of the orchestra who didn't like James," added Gordon as a parting shot when the interview was drawing to a close.

Peter and Chris next called on the house of Inderjit. He lived in a magnificent house. The gabled double front looked out on to an extensive front garden with a well mown lawn and a neat flower bed. This was being tended by someone who was obviously a Sikh.

"Could this be an illegal immigrant?" was a thought that simultaneously passed through Peter and Chris's minds. If Inderjit Singh was aware that James knew he was sheltering illegal immigrants, this would be a possible motive for murder. However, dealing with illegal immigration was not part of Peter and Chris's brief. They would need to pass any suspicions on to the Home Office.

The oak panelled front door was opened by a diminutive little woman of Indian extraction. She was tastefully dressed in a bright sari. They showed her their warrant cards and asked to see Mr. Singh. The lady, whom it turned out was Inderjit's wife, Rajinder Kaur, showed them to a beautifully furnished living room where Inderjit was sitting on a green leather sofa, reading the Times. They declined Rajinder's offer of coffee and something to eat.

Peter and Chris introduced themselves as Inderjit stood up and shook hands.

"I was expecting a visit from you," he said. "I expect that news has got round that I keep snakes. It wasn't one of mine that killed James, though. Yes, I did purchase a green mamba not so long ago but that's still safe in my private animal house. I'll show you round later if you like."

"How do you acquire your snakes?" inquired Peter.

"I work through licensed purveyors of exotic animals." explained Inderjit. "Not anyone can buy these but I have a licence which certifies that the animals are safely and properly housed and fed when in my care."

"I believe you have been to India recently," said Chris. "Do you get many of your animals from abroad?"

Inderjit laughed.

"I hope you don't think I smuggled in a green mamba like the one which bit James. Green mambas come from Africa, anyway, not India. Now had the snake been a cobra….. "

Inderjit changed tack.

"Surprisingly, very few of my animals come from abroad. Most are born in zoos and are surplus to their requirements. These are sold on to exotic animal traders like the one from whom I purchase my animals. Let me show you my paperwork. If you're dealing with dangerous animals, it's very important to have the correct documents available, specially at a time like this when someone has been killed by a snake of unknown origin "

Inderjit went out of the room and returned with a small pile of papers which he handed to Peter. Chris noted the name on the receipt heading of the firm which sourced these animals, 'Clifford Exotic Pets Ltd.' A receipt for payment for a green mamba was included.

They accepted Inderjit's invitation to see his animals and were shown to a sturdily constructed outbuilding in the corner of a large well maintained garden where the azaleas and rhododendrons were still in bloom.

The building contained a large number of vivaria containing tortoises, lizards, small alligators and crocodiles and of course, snakes. In a corner were what the detectives recognised to be snake handling equipment, special gloves, goggles and a specially designed snake handling rod. Chris shuddered when she saw in a separate vivarium, scurrying rodents which were no doubt, live food for the carnivorous reptiles.

Inderjit pointed out the vivarium containing the recently purchased green mamba.

"Fortunately, this was not the one that sadly ended James' life," he said.

Inderjit was a great reptile enthusiast and had they not insisted that they had other duty calls to make, our detectives would have been there the rest of the morning, following a natural history discourse on the strange peculiarities of some of these animals.

As Inderjit showed them out, they told him that they would probably need to return to complete their enquiries.

"I think that Miriam Oldroyd is the next person we need to visit," said Peter.

They called on Miriam, a sharp faced woman whom one might suspect, lacked a sense of humour. She was smartly dressed in a pale green blouse and bottle green trousers which co-ordinated well. Chris recognised these to be from Marks and Spencers' Per Una range. The trousers were part of a medium priced trouser and top combination suit. Miriam lived in a three bedroomed terraced house. The garden was fairly tidy but the lawn would soon need a mow.

"Hallo!" Miriam said abruptly as she answered the door, looking suspiciously hostile to her callers. They showed their warrant cards and were ushered into a well-proportioned kitchen where Miriam gestured them to sit at a table and glared at them from the opposite side.

"I expect that you've called to make enquiries about what happened to James Cummings. Well, I can't tell you much."

"Right in one," responded Peter. "We will still be interested in what you can tell us. Take us through what happened on the journey home."

"Nothing much to tell. We left our cases and instruments to be loaded on to the coach. As a flautist, my instrument is not very big so it can fit quite easily into my travelling case. The journey was uneventful. When we got back to the Black Bear car park, everyone piled out to go for a drink. I don't drink so I stayed outside to keep an eye on the baggage. They all came out about half-an-hour later."

"Did anyone tamper with any of the cases?"

"Not at all. I would have seen them if they did."

"As you almost certainly know by now, James was bitten by a venomous snake from his suitcase. How do you think it got there?"

"I've no idea."

"We think that the snake may have been in another case which was exchanged with James' case at some time during the journey. The only time this could have happened was when you were standing guard over the cases. If no-one else tampered with the cases, you're the only one who could have changed them round. Indeed, as all the cases are similar, all that would be needed would be to swap the labels and the ribbons between James' case and the one containing the snake."

"If I'd done that, how would I have known which case contained the snake?" responded Miriam sharply.

"How indeed?" said Peter, and they paused, giving Miriam time to think of the obvious answer to that question.

"Did you get on well with James?" asked Chris.

"Not at all, but that doesn't mean I killed him. He's a bad driver and he left Sheila, that's my daughter, with a life changing if not life threatening injury when he ran her over. We still don't know if she'll ever be able to walk properly again. The court came to the conclusion that James couldn't have avoided hitting my daughter, but I dispute that. As I've just said, he's a dreadful driver."

"Did you see the accident?"

"No, but I accept my daughter's account. She wouldn't make things up. What's made it worse is that James seemed to think the whole thing was a joke and since the accident, he's referred to me as 'Jaywalker Mum'!"

As they walked away, Peter and Chris recapped on what they had learnt. Chris spoke first.

"It seems very likely that Inderjit is involved. He seems to be the only one who could obtain such a snake. The fact that he had the green mamba he recently ordered in his vivarium doesn't mean that he hadn't another one he could use to kill James."

"Inderjit will obviously argue that he was in the pub with the others at the time we believe the bags were swapped. I think we need to look up 'Clifford Exotic Pets.' and check their records. I saw that you took down the details from Inderjit's receipt. We also need to make a search of Inderjit's house. I've a hunch we'll find some incriminating evidence there."

'Clifford Exotic Pets' was three quarters of an hour's drive away. The detectives explained their business and told the manager on duty, a Mr. Cox, that they were particularly interested in any recent purchases of green mambas. Mr. Cox was most cooperative. He insisted that they were a reputable firm and only sold dangerous animals to customers who had certificates which indicated that they were approved to have custody of such creatures. The records showed that two had been recently sold, one to Inderjit Singh and the other to a Miss. M. Smith, but both were to be delivered to Inderjit's approved house.

Peter and Chris looked satisfyingly at each other. They were obviously getting close to solving the mystery. It appeared that the orders were made by phone and as it was the police making the inquiry, Mr. Cox was prepared to give the details of the credit cards used.

They returned to headquarters and got the necessary permission to trace the source of the credit cards and a search warrant for Inderjit's house. Inderjit seemed unconcerned when he was issued with a search warrant, but clearly became concerned when they discovered two dinner jackets in his wardrobe, the smaller one having a card in the pocket which identified James as a member of the Mossdale orchestra.

Inderjit was told not to leave the area in the immediate future. He said, somewhat menacingly that they might find themselves greeted by a poisonous snake if they came to his house again!

<u>**The Evidence**</u>

James' dinner jacket
This piece of evidence, discovered in Inderjit's wardrobe made him the prime suspect in the case, but how did he manage to swap the case containing the snake with James' case?

The second snake, delivered to Inderjit's house
As Inderjit could show that the snake he had ordered was still in his keeping, he assumed that the police would look elsewhere, not suspecting that the police would be able to trace another order of this venomous reptile which would be discovered to be delivered to his house. The snake could not have been delivered to the Miss M. Smith who had placed the order as her premises were not registered as approved for keeping dangerous animals. There are very few purveyors of dangerous animals and it was not surprising that Miss Smith placed her order with 'Clifford Exotic Pets'.

Receipt for the purchase of the second snake
Christine Powers had taken down the details of this firm from Inderjit's receipts. The fact that the snake ordered by Miss Smith was delivered to

Inderjit' address and the snake was no longer there when the police called was evidence that Miss Smith and Inderjit had worked together to perform this murder, but who was Miss M. Smith? This sounded like a false name.

Identity of Miss Smith

The police's power to investigate bank records in the case of serious crimes like murder was the key to solving Miss Smith's identity. From the credit card details used to purchase the snake, they discovered that Miss Smith's address was the same as Mirian Oldroyd's. Was 'Miss Smith' a false name assumed by Miriam therefore? Not exactly. It was discovered that Smith had been Miriam Oldroyd's maiden name and she retained this name for professional and banking purposes.

The exchange of cases

Once it was clear that Miriam Oldroyd and Inderjit Singh were working together, it was fairly easy to now put together the sequence of events. Inderjit had travelled to Shepherdsford with the snake in his case and any clothing he would need, dinner jacket, etcetera, in Miriam's case. After the performance, Inderjit would have packed his clothes in a plastic bag which he gave to Miriam to put back in her case for the return journey. While the orchestra were celebrating in the Black Bear pub, Miriam had the opportunity to swap the labels on Inderjit and James' cases. Inderjit returned home with James' case and retrieved his clothes from Miriam the following day. Hence, the two dinner jackets discovered in Inderjit's wardrobe. James was of course bitten by the green mamba when he opened his case on his return home.

Motive for the murder
Miriam's motive was her seething hatred for James in view of the injury he had caused her daughter in the road accident. Inderjit would not have been too concerned about being assigned a nickname by James but the realisation that James suspected, or even knew, he was harbouring illegal immigrants, would have been a matter of real concern. Once he discovered that Miriam would be a ready associate in his plan to murder James, he hatched the plan of getting the green mamba into a case James would consider to be his own.

Further investigation by the Home Office confirmed that Inderjit's home was being used as

a safe house for illegal immigrants who were
paying handsomely for this protection.

Chapter 3

<u>A Domestic Violence Event?</u>

Victim – Miranda Foster - 85, Laburnum Terrace, Heronsfield

John Foster, - Miranda's husband
Pauline Barton – 83, Laburnum Terrace
Roy and Helen Woodward – 84, Laburnum Terrace
Lorna Pickering – 87, Laburnum Terrace
Siobhan Kirkpatrick – 89, Laburnum Terrace
Morris Jackson – former work colleague of John Foster, owing him £1,000

The Event

The Incident Response Vehicle (IRV), its blue lights flashing, sped along Laburnum Terrace and braked sharply, stopping outside No. 85. PC Jack Mottram and his female colleague, WPC Wendy Unwin leaped out of the car and ran up the short front garden path to the front door. They didn't have to knock to gain entry. The door was open. A distraught looking man was standing at the entrance. This was John Foster, the houseowner.

He was a tall handsome man. John was wearing his work clothes, a smart navy suit, black polished shoes and a tasteful tie with a blue and white design. The IRV was closely followed by an ambulance.

"Thank you for responding to my call so promptly. I phoned the emergency services no more than three minutes ago. That's when I reported that my wife has been murdered. As I opened the door, this is what I saw!"

John stood to one side to allow the policeman and woman to enter the house. Immediately in front of them lay a woman, face down across the entrance to the kitchen. The back of her head was a mass of blood. Her skull had been caved in. She was clearly dead. By her side lay a bloodied baseball bat.

Jack Mottram drew out his phone and contacted his headquarters.

"PC Jack Mottram speaking. We have just entered 85, Laburnum Terrace in response to a call made at 19:05 hours to investigate a domestic violence incident. On admission to the house, we discovered the victim, a Caucasian female of average height who has been clubbed to death with what appears to be a baseball bat. A man claiming to be her husband is with us now. We'll await the arrival of backup and Scene of Crime Officers and bring the man in to make a statement."

Jack Mottram then turned to John Foster.
"We are responding to a call made about fifteen minutes ago by a woman to report a domestic violence incident at this address. We'll await the arrival of backup officers and then you'll have to accompany us to Police Headquarters to make a full statement. Meanwhile, can you tell us what has happened.?"

"Can I sit down?" said a clearly shaken John.

Jack Mottram accompanied John into the living room while Wendy stood on guard in the hall.

"I was a bit later home from work than usual," started John. "My train arrived at Heronsfield Station at about seven o'clock. I stopped to buy a bunch of flowers at the 24 hours superstore opposite the station for Miranda, that's my wife, and on returning home, this is what I found. I can't tell you any more than that. Whatever's happened? Who's killed my wife? Who'd want to do such a thing? I phoned the police immediately."

Jack Mottram jotted down a few notes.

"I can assure you that this will be most carefully investigated."

He glanced out of the window as another Incident Response Vehicle pulled up. Two policemen got out, entered the house and after a brief conversation with Jack and Wendy, set about their business while Jack and Wendy returned to Police Headquarters with John. John's statement contained no more significant details than that already given to Jack. John was held in custody, pending further investigation.

The Investigation

The following morning, Detective Inspector Peter Sinclair and his sergeant, Chris Powers, entered the headquarters interview room and John Foster was brought in to join them. The Station Officer had told our detectives that this seemed a straightforward case of a domestic argument that had gone too far. The murderer had been caught with a smoking gun (in this case, a bloodied baseball bat). However, in their experience, Peter and Chris knew that things shouldn't just be taken at their face value. Things in police investigations are seldom what they may seem at first.

DI Peter Sinclair turned on the tape recorder, announced the time and what was taking place and started the interrogation.

"Take your time in doing this. Tell us in your own words just what happened yesterday evening."

John gulped.
"I left work a little later than usual, that is, about quarter past six. I had stayed behind to clear up some outstanding paperwork. I normally catch the five thirty from Ramstown but last night I

caught the six-twenty-five which arrived at Heronsfield just after seven. I nipped into the 24 hour superstore just opposite the station to buy a bunch of flowers for Miranda and then walked home. We live just under a quarter-of-an-hour's walk from the station so I must have got home at about quarter past seven. As soon as I opened the door, I saw Miranda lying there at the entrance to the kitchen, the back of her head covered in blood."

John paused to compose himself.

"I went to pick her up but could see that she was dead so I immediately phoned the emergency services."

"Yes," Peter confirmed, "We have your call timed at seventeen minutes past seven. Did anybody see you arrive at the station or go into the superstore?"

"Lots of people but nobody I recognised who could confirm what I've just said. However, Eddy, that's Eddy Brown, the janitor at Arrowsmark where I work, will be able to confirm when I left last night. It would be impossible to get from Arrowsmark to home in less than an hour."

Chris then intervened.

"How did you pay for the flowers? Did you use a card or pay cash?"

"By cash. I only use my card for purchases in excess of £20"

Chris looked across at Peter. No chance then of a time recorded card payment which could be related to John's credit or debit card. However, a record of the payment would have been made. There couldn't have been that many people buying a large bunch of roses at that time in the evening.

Peter continued.

"Can you tell us anything about your neighbours? Is there anyone with whom you or your wife may have had a disagreement recently?"

"I guess it was one of our neighbours who phoned in to report a domestic disturbance. I suppose at this stage in the investigation you cannot tell me who it was. I would say that we get on very well with our neighbours but a couple of things occurred recently which may not have gone down well with the people concerned.

Miranda recently witnessed a hit and run accident in which an old person was badly injured and recognised the driver as one of our neighbours. We agonised about reporting the identity of the driver to the police but Miranda said that we should first give the driver the opportunity of admitting her part in the accident to the police. Miranda called on our neighbour and let her know she had witnessed the accident and that she would rather our neighbour reported what had happened herself before she went to the police. We don't know whether or not the police have received this confession. It was only a couple of days ago that Miranda went to see this neighbour."

Chris noted all this down.

"Can you give us the name of this neighbour?" asked Peter.

"In view of the circumstances, I am prepared to tell you before checking that our neighbour has not already gone to the police herself. It was our next-door neighbour at no. 83, Pauline Barton."

"Are there any other situations which have occurred recently which could have upset a neighbour?"

John pondered.

"Yes, there was another minor event. When Miranda was out shopping on Monday, she called into W H Smith and saw another neighbour pick up quite an expensive pen, put it in her bag and leave the shop without paying. This neighbour is fairly elderly and's really a very simple soul. Miranda caught up with her and told her that if she really needed that pen and couldn't afford it, she would pay for it herself. They returned to Smith's, Miranda paid for the pen and gave it to our neighbour."

"Which neighbour was this?"

"This was Siobhan Kirkpatrick who lives two doors up at No. 89. In the event, no actual crime was committed as the pen was paid for."

"Well, thank you, Mr Foster. I think we'll be able to check out your account and then you'll be free to return home, but as your house is currently "a Scene of Crime', it would be better if you could stay elsewhere for the time being. Have you anywhere you can stay?"

"Yes, I can stay with my daughter in Farmers End which is only half an hour away. She was totally devastated when I phoned to give her this dreadful news. She wanted to come over straight away but I told her not to. There was nothing she could do at this stage. She'll be relieved when she knows that I'm no longer in custody."

Peter want through the formality of verbally stating the time at which the interview had concluded and then turned off the tape-recorder. He signalled to the officer on duty in the interview room who conducted John back to a cell.

Chris turned to Peter.

"It should be a straightforward matter to check this alibi. The janitor's word at Mr. Foster's place of work will do for a start but we can probably do even better if we look through the surveillance cameras at the station and the superstore."

Sure enough, John Foster could be clearly identified on both the tape from the camera which surveyed the turnstiles through which passengers passed when leaving Heronsfield Station and that from the superstore camera. A phone call to Eddy Brown, the janitor at Arrowsmark confirming when John Foster left work was sufficient to enable John Foster to be released from custody. He was asked to give his contact number at his daughter's and asked not to travel far as it was likely that he'd be needed for further questioning.

The next stage of the investigation was to visit the crime scene. They crossed the blue tape across the gate of 85, Laburnum Terrace and were met by a police constable on duty who showed them in. Their attention immediately focused on a white outline which marked where the body had fallen across the entrance to the kitchen.

"There was no sign of forced entry," explained the constable "so it would appear that the victim had allowed access to someone who followed her towards the kitchen and then clubbed her to death from behind. A blood-stained baseball bat was found beside the body."

Peter and Chris surveyed the house. It was neat, clean and tidy with no sign of any other domestic turbulence. A number of unopened letters lay on the kitchen table, three of which proclaimed on the envelopes the charities from which they originated, 'Christian Aid', 'Save the Children' and 'Global Care'. As well as family photos, the walls were covered with large pictures of beautiful scenery which included Bible texts. Among the ornaments on the mantlepiece was a fish symbol, which was further evidence to indicate that the householders were Christian.

After thanking the constable on duty, Peter and Chris decided to call in at the mortuary, Dr Edward Cooper, the pathologist was there to meet them.

"No doubt about the cause of death," he announced. "The victim's skull had been fractured from blows to the back of the head, but the state of the body indicates that death had occurred some time before the police received the phone call informing them that a case of domestic violence needed to be investigated. Rigour mortis had already started to take place."

He pointed to a blood-stained baseball bat on a bench.

"This was the murder weapon. The blood stains match the victim's but the perpetrator of this crime must have been wearing gloves. There were no fingerprints."

The detectives both thought to themselves that if this was indeed an unpremeditated crime of passion, the murderer would have been unlikely to have put on gloves first. They thanked Edward for the useful information he'd given them.

"I think we now need to call on the neighbours to discover what they had seen and heard," Peter declared. "I think that the woman who phoned in to report the incident should be our first port of call."

They arrived at 83 Laburnum Terrace. A battered red mini with rust showing through the paintwork was parked outside.

"How did this get through its MOT?" they both thought.

Chris rang the bell and the door was opened by a sour faced woman in her late fifties. She was wearing a grubby housecoat with a faded floral pattern, well-worn green slippers and crumpled stockings.

Peter didn't have to make a formal introduction. Pauline Barton spoke first.

"You'll be the police making enquiries about that dreadful incident next door. I'm Mrs Barton. I called the police as soon as I realised something terrible was going on. Come on into the living room."

She ushered them into a drab parlour which hadn't been properly dusted for weeks. Outdated copies of 'Woman and Home' and 'The Lady' were on a badly scratched coffee table in front of what once must have been an elegant fireplace.

Pauline gestured them to sit on a grubby sofa while she sat on one of the badly worn leather armchairs which was part of a three-piece suite. More magazines were piled on the third chair which made up the suite.

Peter asked Pauline Barton to explain as carefully as she could what had happened during the late afternoon of the previous day which led to her phoning the police.

"Not much to tell. I heard such a commotion next door, a man and a woman's voices – it must have been John and Miranda - shouting at each other. This went on for no more than ten minutes, and then I heard a loud thump. I realised that something dreadful must have happened and so I phoned the police. You know the rest."

"Did you phone the police immediately you knew something was going wrong?" asked Peter.

"Yes, of course."

Chris looked up from her notebook at Peter who didn't return the glance.

"Why are you sure that it was John and Miranda rowing? Did you see anyone else coming into the house?"

"Well, I don't sit looking out of my window all day so I didn't see any comings or goings but who else could it have been but John and Miranda?"

"Did they often have rows?" interjected Chris.

"Not that I've ever heard them, but I'm not in my house listening for them all day."

"Did they seem to get on well as a couple?" asked Peter.

"Tolerably well but I'm sure they had their ups and downs like everybody does."

"Can you tell us anything else about what happened yesterday?" asked Chris.

"No. I've told you all I know. I phoned at five past seven and the police car arrived a quarter of an hour later. When another police car arrived and the police went into the house, I saw John being escorted to the first police car which drove away.

An ambulance had arrived just after the first police car and quite sometime later, a stretcher, which I assumed was carrying Miranda's body, was loaded on to the ambulance. Some of the police at the house were wearing what looked to me like white boiler suits."

Chris then intervened with a question.

"Did you get on well with your neighbours? Did you have any arguments?"

"I would say tolerably well but Miranda was a bit of a nosey so-and-so. She was very disparaging about my driving and told me when she'd seen ma driving badly but she'd got the wrong car. I was nowhere near the place at the time when she claimed she'd spotted me doing a dangerous manoeuvre."

Peter and Chris independently wondered how anyone could mistake the battered car they'd seen outside.

"Well, thank you, Mrs. Barton," said Peter. "I expect that we'll be round again with more questions."

"There's not much more I'll be able to tell you," said Joan Barton as a parting shot as she showed Peter and Chris out.

Peter mentioned something that Chris had independently picked up during the interview, that there was a disparity between Mrs. Barton's timing of events and the time of death suggested by Edward, the pathologist.

"This is something which will need to be explained," he said.

They proceeded three doors up to 87 on the other side of the Fosters' house. The door was opened by a smart looking woman in her early thirties. On being shown the warrant cards the woman invited them into her front room. She introduced herself as Lorna Pickering and explained that they were lucky to find her in as she worked part-time and most mornings, she would have been doing admin work at 'George, Ellison and George', the local firm of solicitors. Today, however, the office had been closed for decorating. The information Lorna could provide was negative but helpful just the same. 'Yes', she had been at home at seven o'clock on Tuesday afternoon but

'No', she'd heard nothing and was unaware that anything unusual was happening next door until she heard the police car (Incident Response Vehicle) arrive at the house. She was shocked by what had happened. She really got on well with John and Miranda who were such a devoted couple. 'No', she didn't believe a lovely man like John could possibly have murdered his wife.

After thanking Lorna, the detectives crossed the road to No. 84, the home of Roy and Helen Woodward. As with Lorna, the first they were aware of an incident was when the police car turned up, and like Lorna, they saw the Fosters as a model married couple. It was inconceivable that John could possibly have murdered Miranda. Roy and Helen attended the same church as John and Miranda and knew them in some depth. They were exemplary members not only of the church but of society. No-one had ever heard them speak an angry word or had a cross word with them. They were always willing to help anyone, regardless of any inconvenience to themselves. Miranda ran the Sunday School and organised a baby-sitting rota for church members. John led the Bible class for children of secondary school age.

Chris asked Roy and Helen if they were aware of any problems being experienced by the Fosters at this time.

Roy mentioned that Miranda was a bit anxious that some money John had lent to a former work colleague had not yet been repaid as they were needing the money to replace their worn-out bed. Otherwise, there was nothing they could think of.

Peter and Chris had their suspicions that Joan Barton was not being completely honest but apart from the disparity in timing, they had no really positive evidence to link her to Miranda's death.

Peter remembered that John had mentioned another neighbour whom Miranda had helped out when it appeared she had been stealing a pen from W H Smith. They decided to call on Siobhan Kirkpatrick who lived two doors up at No. 89. As they entered the hall, Chris's eyes were drawn to the unusual design of the overcoat hanging in the hall. It was pale brown with prominent black zig-zag markings. Siobhan was a small, timid-looking woman who was probably in her late sixties. She wore a woolly jumper two sizes too big over a long tweed skirt. Siobhan showed them into her living room which had peeling wallpaper and pictures reminiscent of yesteryear, copies of pre-Raphaelite paintings and Sir Edwin Landseer's 'Monarch of the Glen'.

On being asked if she had heard anything unusual the previous Tuesday, Siobhan was very forthcoming.

"Oh yes, I heard a tremendous row coming from No. 85. A man and a woman shouting. Crockery being thrown about. What sounded like furniture being broken."

"Can you give us any estimate of the time this took place?" asked Peter.

"Yes, it started at five-past-seven and went on for half an hour."

"Did you get on well with your neighbours?" asked Chris.

"Oh, yes. Miranda was very kind to me."

"Did you ever have any arguments with them?" Chris added as a follow-up question.

"No, never. We were all very friendly together."

"Well, I don't think we need to trouble you any further for the time-being, Mrs. Kirkpatrick but we'll be calling again with some follow up questions," said Peter as he got to his feet and Siobhan showed them out.

Chris felt that Peter was dissatisfied with the interview as she was herself.

"She's obviously lying," said Peter. "The timing she gave would take us beyond the time the police arrived at No. 85, and there was no sign of broken furniture or crockery in the house. On the contrary, No. 85 was extremely tidy."

"Did you notice the coat in the hall?" asked Chris.

"I can't say that I did," replied Peter. "Is that important."

"You don't see many coats like that but I know that I've recently seen one of that design, but where? Then it came to me. There was a woman wearing a coat like that in the station surveillance video.”

“Let’s go back and examine the footage again,” said Peter.
They returned to the station.

Yes, sure enough, standing next to a pillar so she wouldn’t be easily seen by the passengers passing through the ticket barrier was a woman wearing a coat just like Siobhan’s. Indeed, it almost certainly was Siobhan. She was speaking to someone on her mobile phone.

The couple immediately returned to 89, Laburnum Terrace.

Siobhan was surprised to see them again and as before, they were shown into her living room.

Peter spoke quite sternly.

“When we called this afternoon, you clearly told us a pack of lies. You were seen at the station at just after seven o’clock. There was no crockery or broken furniture at No. 85. Your neighbour at No. 87 heard nothing and I rather think she has better hearing than you. We are dealing with a murder! Unless you start to tell us the truth, you could be in very serious trouble, very serious trouble indeed."

Siobhan's lip trembled and she started to whimper.

"Joan said that Miranda was going to report her to the police for bad driving and me for shoplifting. She'd lose her driving licence and I'd be put in prison. She said that if the police called at their house when they were having a big row, that would stop them from being able to report us. She asked me to go to the station and phone her as soon as I saw John leaving the station so that she could phone the police to arrive just after John returned home. I didn't know that John was going to kill Miranda."

The logic of Siobhan's statement escaped Peter and Chris, but Siobhan was not a logical thinker. She was clearly a very gullible person with a simple mind who could be so easily manipulated by a stronger personality like Joan Barton.

Siobhan continued to sob. Chris spoke in a more conciliatory tone.

"Don't worry. I can reassure you that John did not kill Miranda. Someone else did. What you have told us will be of great help in finding out who did. Next time you are asked questions by the police, be sure to tell the truth. They'll soon find out if you are lying as we did this time. You could have got yourself into more trouble that you can imagine."

They left Siobhan's house. She was still wiping her eyes as they walked down the path.

"I think it's pretty plain that Joan Barton murdered Miranda Foster to avoid being reported for the hit and run accident," said Peter.

The first thing the detectives did when they returned to the station was to log into the driving records data base. They discovered that Joan had a number of convictions and had attended three drivers' safety awareness courses to avoid getting the points on her licence which would otherwise have taken her over the limit and disqualified her

95

from driving. She was currently two points short of the critical twenty mark.

"We need a bit more evidence to get a cast iron case against Mrs. Barton," added Chris. "I think we might be able to find out who bought the baseball bat. It was obviously quite new."

There were only two sports shops in Heronsfield. 'Aston Trainer and Sportswear' specialised mainly in sports kit and didn't stock baseball bats. However, 'Ambrose Athletics' had sold three baseball bats over the last couple of days, two to a couple of teenagers and one to a middle-aged woman. She struck them as an unlikely customer for this item. No card had been used. It was a cash transaction.

Peter asked the store manager who had actually conducted the sale if he could recognise the person to whom he had sold the bat and if anyone else in the shop might be able to make this recognition. My cashier who dealt with the money probably could and so could my assistant, Graham, who wrapped the purchase. Peter asked them if they were prepared to assist in an identity parade they were aiming to set up.

It wasn't too difficult to find five other women of a similar height, build and appearance to Joan to take place in this parade. When summoned to come along, Joan Barton at first protested. She couldn't imagine what she might have been identified as doing but when she was told that she was a suspect and this could help eliminate her from the police enquiry, she readily agreed to come along. Needless to say, all three employees at 'Ambrose Athletics', when peering at the parade from a vantage point concealed from the paraded members, immediately recognised Joan Barton as the person who had bought the baseball bat two days earlier. Joan admitted buying the baseball bat but couldn't explain why or say where the baseball bat was now. She was immediately arrested and charged with the murder of Miranda Foster.

"Well done for thinking up the idea of having an identity parade to identify the murderer," said Peter to Chris afterwards. "Joan Barton obviously thought she could exploit the fact that Siobhan was simple-minded to get her to take part in the way she did, but a simple-minded person isn't going to provide much protection for the guilty party when under interrogation, especially when they have no idea of what's really going on. I don't think there will be any need to take action against Siobhan. She wasn't an accomplice in the normal sense of the word.

<u>**The Evidence**</u>

John's alibi
This was supported by surveillance camera footage and Eddy Brown, the Janitor at Arrowsmark, confirmed, not only the time that John had left work for home, but testified that he hadn't left work at any other time throughout the day.

Disparity in timing
The fact that the timing of Pauline Barton's phone call reporting the incident did not agree with the pathologist's estimated time of death needed to be explained but in the absence of other neighbours' corroboration, no explanation was immediately available. The fact that the other neighbours had heard nothing was also significant.

Money owed to John
John explained that he had lent £1,000 to a former work colleague, Morris Jackson, and that Miranda had been to his mind, unnecessarily anxious about it being repaid. Morris was a completely reliable person and this couldn't be connected with the investigation in hand in any way.

Evidence provided by Siobhan
Siobhan was a simple minded individual who had been manipulated by a stronger personality into doing something whose purpose she didn't understand but had been deceived that she needed to do this in order to avoid prison. She didn't have the wit to lie to the police with a credible story which the detectives might have difficulty in exposing as lies. Having had her lies exposed, Siobhan reverted to telling the truth which gave Peter and Chris all the information needed.

Joan Barton's driving record.
The fact that Joan Barton had accumulated sufficient points to put her at risk of being disqualified from driving, and the threat represented by the possibility that Miranda would report the hit and run accident, proved sufficient motive for murder.

The baseball bat
The final conclusive evidence for Joan's guilt was provided when she was identified as the person who had bought the baseball bat.

Epilogue

Peter and Chris felt really sorry for John Foster with whom they felt a natural affinity. They therefore arranged to meet him socially to talk over his recent experience. They met at the White Lion, Heronsfield, for lunch. The White Lion was a well-appointed hostelry, located by a picturesque stretch of the River Itchen.

John was full of praise for the way they'd carried out their investigation, identifying the person who had murdered Miranda in a very short space of time. They asked him what were his feelings towards Joan Barton and Siobhan Kirkpatrick.

"I feel very sorry for Siobhan. She's a simple soul. She would have had no idea what was afoot when Joan recruited her to make that phone call. I'm glad that no action is going to be taken against Siobhan. Joan? – well I'm appalled that she should exploit the simplicity of an elderly woman like Siobhan to further her evil deed. What's my feeling towards her? The code of conduct by which we live requires us to love others, even our enemies. Well, you can't conjure up deep love out of nothing. There are a few people you can love naturally. There are others you can really like, but this falls short of deep love. There are others around us whom we don't even like so how can we love them? What we can do is to behave in a loving way towards them, and this includes people who have done us great injury like Joan. No, I can't bring myself to hate Joan or anyone else for that matter. I feel terribly sorry for her and the burden she will now have to bear. She's had a hard life. She was devastated when her husband walked out on her some years ago and she's never got over it. It's poisoned her life but I'm not going to give in to hate and let it poison my life as I've seen it do to others. No, I want Joan to know that I bear her no ill feeling and am even prepared to help her if she needs me at this difficult time, but I don't really know what help I can give.

There's something else which you wouldn't have known and it's unlikely that your police pathologist would have picked it up. Miranda was suffering from terminal ovarian cancer. This is a silent killer, a disease which creeps up and often shows no symptoms until it's beyond a cure. This was the case with Miranda. When diagnosed, the prognosis was not good. Even with chemo and radio therapy, her life expectancy was no more than a year, perhaps eighteen months. She has now been spared the physical suffering which will come as the disease advances and I, the mental anguish of seeing Miranda suffer.

At a time like this, my faith is a great source of strength and comfort to me. I have an assurance that many lack, that in due course, Miranda and I will meet again in the life to come. Meanwhile, I can look back on a really wonderful marriage which many would say was made in heaven. I have no regrets that we missed out on anything really important in life.

I have seen various jobs with missionary societies which would suit me well, but even allowing for the loss of income involved which was not too important an issue, the work itself would not have suited Miranda. I now have the freedom to investigate whether or not a future for me lies down that path."

Peter and Chris felt very moved but at the same time, very reassured by what John Foster had shared. He was a person with whom they'd want to keep in touch although this was contrary to police protocol. They mutually wished one another every blessing for the future as they parted after what had been a very special and memorable meal.

Chapter 4

Teacher Day at Carickhampton School

Victim - Callum Moncaster, - Chemistry
teacher

Jacob Harmsworth,   - Headmaster
Angus McDonald,   - P.E. teacher
Philippa Jones   - Games mistress
Florence Brimstone,   - English teacher
Jack Counsellor,   - Maths teacher
Philip Smith,   - Registrar and finance
officer
Eric Townsend,   - Laboratory technician
Joe Shoesmith,   - Supply teacher
covering for Callum
Moncaster

The Event

It was a teacher day, a day when the staff could get on with jobs and hold meetings which were better done at times when there was no distraction from the ever-pressing demands of the children they were there to teach.

Carickhampton School was a run-of-the-mill comprehensive school, located in Hampshire. It ran fairly smoothly under the leadership of Jacob Harmsworth who had been Headmaster there for the past four years. Like most schools, Carickhampton had its problems, not least of which was antagonism among staff members – or more correctly, antagonism created by one particular member of staff. Callum Moncaster who taught chemistry was not popular. He was a loner. He said insulting things to other staff members, particularly the women. He exploited any problem of which he became aware to create maximum difficulty for his fellow teachers.

The games mistress, Philippa Jones entered the staff room dressed in her usual tracksuit bearing a badge that showed she had once played netball for Kent. Callum called out to Philippa from the other side of the room.

"I saw you conducting a coaching session on the netball court last week and thought that a scraggy woman like yourself should be careful about exposing too much of her body. With your muscular definition and ribs that protrude so that they can be counted, you would be more use modelling for an anatomy lesson in the biology department than sporting yourself in a semi-undressed state on the netball court!"

Florence Brimstone, the English teacher rose to Philippa's support.

"Oh, shut up. Callum. Philippa's not scraggy. Most of us would be proud to have a figure like hers."

"Of course you would," retorted Callum. "You need to go on a 'Weight Watchers' course to get rid of all that flab you carry around with you."

The two women didn't rise to the bait and seemed to ignore this remark as they started a conversation with each other about other matters.

The next person to enter the staff room was Angus McDonald, head of the P.E. department. There had long been a feud between Angus and Callum who considered that the P.E. department received a disproportionately large share of the school equipment budget.

"I don't know how you justify spending all that money on equipment for the gym. We're here to prepare the kids for a world of work where they'll need to earn money. Good careers lie in the sciences. The country is crying out for competent chemists. There's no great demand for gymnasts. The school's money should be concentrated in the departments which are preparing the kids for the jobs the country needs to be done, not departments which are just concerned with recreational activities."

Before Angus could reply, Jacob Harmsworth entered the staffroom to inform them that the general staff meeting would not be held until three that afternoon in the school library and he suggested that staff should return to their departmental areas to prepare the statistics he needed for the presentation he was due to give to the governors.

The teachers started to move out of the staffroom. As they dispersed, Jacob asked Angus if he could meet him in his office at two o'clock. So it was, at the appointed time, Angus joined Jacob for a pre-arranged meeting about the prospects of getting the school sports teams near the top of the county ratings during the year. They were deep in conversation when a loud report was heard. They rushed into the corridor.

"Where did that sound come from?" demanded Jacob of Jack Counsellor, the maths teacher who had just emerged into the corridor from another classroom where he had been working.

"I think it came from the prep room."

The prep room was the room adjoining the Chemistry laboratory which was Callum Moncaster's headquarters. Jacob tried the door. It was locked. He went to get his master key but couldn't open the door. It was locked from the inside and the key was still inside the lock. There was another door from the prep room which opened directly into the laboratory. This too was locked but Jacob was able to open the door with his master key. There, lying face down on the floor was Callum, a bullet wound in his head and a gun on the floor next to him. By this time, other staff had gathered. Jacob ushered them out through the door which opened into the lab and locked the door as he left himself. He immediately phoned the emergency services.

A constable from the local station arrived, looked at the body and phoned for backup. While he was taking a statement from Jacob, an ambulance and other police, including Scene of Crime Officers, arrived. Photos were taken and the body was removed to the police mortuary along with the other main piece of evidence, the gun. Apparent suicides are seldom taken at their face value until further examination has been carried out.

The Investigation

Peter and Chris were called on to investigate this apparent suicide. They made the mortuary their first port of call. Dr Edward Cooper rose from his desk as they entered. Edward was a tall distinguished looking man. He wore rimless spectacles hooked over ears just below his remaining tufts of grey hair. Although his job could get very messy, he always wore a spotless white laboratory coat. He had well laundered spares hanging from the wall of his office into which he changed, should his coat become stained during the course of his work. On first acquaintance, Dr Cooper may have been taken as an overly serious man with no sense of humour, but those who knew him well knew otherwise. He often had a droll comment to make about some of the messy situations in which his work involved him.

"What time was the gun report heard?" asked Edward. "Two thirty? Well, like some of the other cases in which you have been involved recently, I can tell you from the state of the body, the victim died before two-thirty, I would say by two or three hours."

Edward took them over to the slab where the body was laid out to indicate another piece of relevant information. He removed the top part of the sheet covering the cadaver. Chris shuddered as the expressionless face came into view. Although she had had to deal with dead bodies in her line of duty, the sight of a corpse in the morgue was one she didn't think she'd ever get used to.

"When people commit suicide by shooting themselves, they invariably fire through the mouth or the temple. This shot was fired a little way round the head towards the back. It wouldn't be impossible to shoot oneself from this angle but it would have been unnecessarily awkward."

"Several people heard the gun go off at two thirty," mentioned Peter. "Whatever was going on?"

"People heard what sounded like a gun report," explained Edward. "These days, electronic devices are available to make whatever noise you want at whatever time you would like."

"Yes," added Chris. "My niece has a device she calls 'Alexa'. They have an app called 'spotify'

<u>and she can ask it to play any music she wants at</u> any time. My brother even uses it as an alarm clock.”

“So, you see,” said Edward, “if someone wanted to make it seem as if a gun had gone off at a pre-arranged time, it would be quite easy to set up. It’s possible that the person who did set this up hasn’t had an opportunity to remove it before the room was sealed as an incident site. You may well find that it’s still there.”

“So, when the fatal shot was actually fired,” deduced Peter, “no-one heard it because the gun was fitted with a silencer. Although a silencer doesn’t completely silence a gun, when used in a closed room with no-one else particularly near, nothing would have been noticed.”

“Exactly,” Edward concluded.

He then showed them the gun which had been found beside the body. The finger- prints on the gun were the victim’s but the gun had probably been placed into his hand post mortem.

Peter and Chris thanked Edward for all this very relevant information and then proceeded to make their way to Carickhampton School. Parents had been informed not to send their children to school for the next couple of days as the death of a member of staff on the premises was being investigated. Staff were asked to attend as usual.

"What a bad business," said Jacob Harmsworth as the detectives were ushered into his office. Jacob looked very much a headmaster. He had an authoritive air and was smartly dressed in a brown suit with matching tie. "I know that Callum, that is, Mr. Moncaster, wasn't liked but he seemed to be a pretty thick-skinned sort of fellow. I wouldn't have thought that knowing he was unpopular would have caused him to take his own life."

Peter and Chris sat at the seats opposite Jacob's desk to which he had gestured them,

"Things aren't as straightforward as that," said Peter. "Facts have emerged which mean we're investigating this as a case of murder."

Jacob looked shocked.

"What facts?"

"We're not at liberty to disclose those at present. We'll first have to interview the staff who were in the building at the time. Can it be arranged that we see them all individually?"

"Of course."

"We'll need to know everyone's whereabouts, not just at the time of the shooting but from midday onwards. Where were you, Mr. Harmsworth?"

"I went for lunch at midday. I would say that between twelve and one, I saw most of the staff in the refectory. At one o'clock, I returned to my office. I had a short meeting, about ten minutes, with Philip, that's Mr. Philip Smith our registrar, and then, at two thirty, I met Angus, Angus McDonald who's in charge of Physical Education. Our meeting had almost finished when at about two thirty, we heard the gun go off. We rushed into the corridor just as Jack Counsellor was leaving his room to find out what had happened. He thought the sound had come from the prep room which adjoins the chemistry laboratory. The door was locked and I couldn't get in from the corridor side, even with my master key, as there was a key in the other side of the lock. We were able to get in from the door which opens into the lab, and there, as you know, we found poor Callum, dead on the floor."

Jacob arranged for the detectives to have the use of a small office where they interviewed each member of staff individually. Most of them had alibis to account for where they were at two-thirty, the supposed time of the shooting, but their whereabouts between midday and two thirty were all a bit hazy. No-one had seen Callum enter the prep room but two members of staff who had reason to go to the prep room had found the door locked and no-one answered when they knocked. All of them had anecdotes about Callum's rudeness. Every member of staff had had insults directed at themselves, but these were becoming a bit of a joke which even had a unifying effect on the staff. It seems that no-one had felt offended to the extent that they would kill Callum.

One of the people interviewed was Eric Townsend, the laboratory technician. If anyone had a motive for getting rid of Callum, it would have been Eric whose life, it would appear from reports, both from Eric himself and other members of staff, was made a misery by Callum, his line manager. Why hadn't he been in the prep room or the laboratory on the day Callum died? Jacob had arranged for Eric to go to Southampton on an errand for the school, an excursion which had taken Eric most of the day.

Peter and Chris had a specially interesting interview with the school finance officer, Philip Smith. He could site lots of examples where Callum had come to him for information which he knew Callum would use to create trouble with other staff members. Callum had a particular feud with Angus McDonald whom he considered was receiving a disproportionate share of the resources, needed for the day to day running of the school, for the Physical Education department. He had recently asked for a sight of all the paperwork associated with orders made for PE equipment, invoices, receipts, delivery notes, etc. Philip had had to spend some time in gathering all this information and would have passed them on to Callum had not he died the day before his getting the final documents together. He now had a complete dossier which he was prepared to pass on to the police. It appeared that Callum may have been fully justified in being dissatisfied with the way decisions were made by Jacob in the way school finances were handled.

Before leaving the school, Peter and Chris went to have a look round the prep room which was sealed for normal entry. A Scene of Crime Officer was still working there. The shelves and cupboards in the room were crowded with chemicals, apparatus, catalogues, anything which might find its place in a school science department. It was an untidy mess but Chris's eagle eyes spotted something of significance. It was a small cylindrical device unobtrusively placed on a shelf among other apparatus. The policeman on duty there confirmed that it was a device like 'echodot' which could be programmed to broadcast music or other sounds as a result of a verbal command. Yes, a delay could be programmed into this particular device between a command being given and the response being made. They carefully put this device into a plastic bag and returned it to the forensic lab for investigation including dusting it for fingerprints.

At the end of the day which had been spent in carrying out intensive interviews with all the staff members, Peter and Chris felt quite exhausted. Everyone had a minor motive for wanting to see the end of Callum Moncaster but nothing had shown up which was a clear pointer as to who might have committed this crime.

"We'll go home and have a good night's sleep," suggested Peter. "That might clear our heads by the morning and some ideas may come to us."

He shook the thick bundle of papers which were photocopies of the original financial transaction documents which Philip Smith had gathered.

"These may contain some indication of improper financial practice at the school which could be a possible motive for murder. The best people to check these out are not ourselves but the team which deals with financial fraud and so called, white collar crime. In the morning, I'll pass these on to them for scrutiny."

The Financial Fraud Team came up with some interesting answers within three days of receiving the documents. Chief Inspector Henry Longstaff of the Financial Fraud Team phoned Peter to let him know what they had discovered. Some of the payments had been made to genuine providers of sports and gymnastic equipment but many of them had been made to a business called 'Modern Sports Equipment'. This was registered as a holding company and in spite of its name, did not actually handle any sports equipment at all! Its director was Jacob Harmsworth. It had to be set up as a proper company in order to be able to open a bank account. A large number of orders were placed with this firm for items like trampolines, vaulting horses, exercise mats, goal posts and nets, cricket bats, hockey sticks and balls for use in any of these sports. The invoices were provided on professional looking forms with a coloured header and what turned out to be a fictitious address. A note on the invoice required that payments should be made by bank transfer. Angus McDonald had signed the invoices as goods received and these had been countersigned by Jacob Harmsworth so that they could be processed for payment. Examination of the bank statements of 'Modern Sports Equipment' showed that large payments had been transferred from the school to this business and also, that significant sums of money had been paid by bank transfer from this company's account to the accounts of Jacob Harmsworth and Angus McDonald.

Chief Inspector Henry Longstaff of the Financial Fraud Team reported to Peter and Chris how busy his team were these days dealing with ever expanding white collar crime. The particular fraud they had just uncovered at Carickhampton School was typical of an increasingly common form of fraud in which big businesses were paying out on false invoices signed off by trusted senior members of staff. The many cases like this one, actually unearthed, were probably only the tip of a very big iceberg.

Peter and Chris felt enormously encouraged by this finding. They now had the motive for murder but they only had evidence so far to mount a fraud case. They would need to do more to link Jacob Harmsworth and Angus McDonald with Callum Moncaster's murder.

Peter outlined to Chris a plan he had thought out which might smoke out the guilty parties.

"Do you think the Chief Constable will approve of this?" queried Chris, knowing that they would be sailing close to the wind.

"If this leads to a result, the Chief Constable will be delighted. I know he likes risk takers," was Peter's confident assertion.

Peter and Chris arranged with Jacob to visit the school again during the lunchbreak when the classrooms would be unoccupied. They told him that just wandering through the classrooms might give them some inspiration in a case they were struggling with. They asked Jacob to remain in his office so that they could contact him immediately should any idea come to mind. Jacob agreed to this, He couldn't see how wandering through the classrooms would be of any help at all but this was up to the police.

On the appointed Tuesday, they arrived at the school just before midday with a search warrant and the echodot device which had been prepared in a special way to fulfil their plan. The receptionist informed Jacob of their arrival and they were ushered to his office. Jacob stood up to meet them.

"The kids are on their lunch break," he said quite affably. "Please feel free to wander where you will round the school. I hope you find what you are looking for."

They thanked Jacob for extending this help.

"A strange thing came up when we examined Mr Moncaster's body," said Peter. "We understand that Mr Moncaster was a non-smoker yet we found this in his pocket. Does this mean anything to you?"

Peter took out from his pocket a shiny cigarette case and handed it to Jacob. Jacob took the case, turned it over, opened it to see if there were any cigarettes inside. It was empty. He clicked it shut and handed it back to Peter and shrugged his shoulders.

"I've never seen this before. I can't think what Callum had it for. As you say, he was a non-smoker."

They thanked Jacob and then went across the corridor to the prep room which was just a few steps along from being directly opposite the headmaster's office. Here, they encountered a Mr Shoesmith, the supply teacher who was filling in for the deceased Mr Moncaster until a permanent replacement could be appointed. They asked Mr Shoesmith if he could sit as unobtrusively as possible in a corner of the prep room and observe what happened over the next half-hour. Chris then replaced the echodot device in exactly the same place on the crowded shelf as it had been when she had taken it a few days earlier. They went out, leaving the door of the prep room on the corridor side, partly open.

Peter had good spatial sense and had assessed the basic layout of the school very well from his previous visits. After leaving the prep room, Peter and Chris made their way to a classroom on the first floor which was on the opposite side of a small quadrangle on to which Jacob's office on the ground floor also faced. From this vantage point they could look down across to the headmaster's study where the back of Jacob could be clearly seen, sitting at his desk, doing paperwork.

They sat there for about ten minutes, hoping their idea would work out as planned. Suddenly, a loud voice rang out from the prep room.

"I have your silencer. How much will you pay to get it back and silence me?"

Jacob jumped out of his seat and dashed across to the prep room, returning in seconds to his office, clutching the echodot device. He sat at his desk, withdrew a key from the tray drawer at the top of the desk, unlocked the first drawer down, rummaged around this drawer for a few moments and then closed and locked the drawer.

Peter contacted the backup team which was waiting just outside the school gate and Peter and Chris returned to Jacob's study.

"We have a search warrant to look around this school and we would now like to examine your study."

"Go ahead," said Jacob, looking distinctly worried. He looked even more worried when Peter retrieved the key to the top drawer of his desk and after rummaging round for a few seconds, pulled out the silencer.

"Jacob Harmsworth," began Peter, "I am arresting you for the murder of Callum Moncaster. You do not need to say anything, but if you do, it may be used as evidence at your trial."

This was the cue for the two back up officers to enter the office, handcuff Jacob and lead him away.

There was just one more thing for Peter and Chris to check out. They went back to the prep room and asked Mr Shoesmith what he had seen and heard.

"Well, that device you put on the shelf suddenly burst out with a message about a silencer, Mr. Harmsworth dashed in, snatched it off the shelf and returned to his office."

"Thank you, Mr Shoesmith," said Chris. "Was it silent when Mr Harmsworth came in? Had it stopped speaking? How did Mr. Harmsworth know where it was?"

"Oh yes, it had certainly finished when Mr. Harmsworth came in, but he knew exactly what he was looking for and where it was without having to search around."

"Thank you again, Mr Shoesmith. That's been very helpful."

As they left the school, Chris expressed to Peter a remaining concern about the case they had just solved.

"What about Mr. McDonald?" queried Chris. "He was very much involved in this. He must have known about the murder plan."

"Sadly, we can't even arrest him as an accomplice," said Peter. "The statements made by the staff when we interviewed them, indicate that Angus had witnesses to confirm an alibi that he was nowhere near the prep room over the few hours when the murder took place. However, he will certainly be given a stiff sentence for his involvement in the financial fraud which we have uncovered.

The Evidence

The echodot type device

This was obviously placed by the murderer to simulate a gunshot at a time when he or she had arranged an alibi. The murderer would not have taken into account that a pathologist would be able to estimate an approximate time of death from the state of the body, provided not too much time had elapsed. The device would not have been obvious among shelves of untidily arranged scientific apparatus, but knowing what she was looking for, Chris had managed to locate the item. The fingerprints on the device would be a crucial piece of evidence but these would be useless unless Peter and Chris could obtain a set of fingerprints from prime suspects.

The Financial Transaction Documents

These clearly indicated that a financial fraud was being operated. The need to prevent the discovery of this fraud provided a motive for murder.

The absence of Eric Townsend

Normally, Eric would have either been in the chemistry laboratory or the prep room which would have inhibited any attempt to enter the prep room unnoticed and murder Callum. The fact that it was Jacob Harmsworth who had sent Eric on an errand to Southampton was evidence of the premeditated aspect of this murder.

A stratagem to obtain the final pieces of evidence.

The scheme worked out by Peter and Chris, unearthed three pieces of crucial evidence.

Jacob Harmsworth's fingerprints on the cigarette case that the detectives had handed Jacob to examine could be matched to fingerprints on the echodot device.

The fact that Jacob Harmsworth knew exactly where this device was without needing to carefully search through an untidy prep room full of equipment, indicated that he was the one who had planted the device in the first place. This was used to simulate a gunshot noise at a time when Jacob Harmsworth had an alibi.

The discovery of the silencer in Jacob's desk which would have been needed to shoot Callum Moncaster without attracting attention was a final conclusive piece of evidence, proving Jacob's guilt.

Chapter 5

<u>Murder at the Boardroom</u>

Victim – Sir Tobias Trelawny, Chairman and
        managing director of 'Chemical
        Solutions Ltd'

Board Members
        Lancelot Ripon
        Ferdinand Jones
        Colonel Colin Temporley
        Henry Masterton
        Clive Mountjoy
        Christopher Hammond
        Terence Rastrick
        Fergus McIntyre

        Geoffery Monroe (clerk to the
                board of governors)

Julie English, Coffee Maid
Edward Jones – Manager of Henley
           Pharmaceuticals Ltd.
Dr Stephen Johnson – Chief chemist at
           Henley Pharmaceuticals Ltd.
Penelope Halfpenny – Shareholder in
           Camden and Rush Ltd.

The Event

The board-meeting was fraught. Members of the board of Chemical Solutions Ltd. were debating whether or not it was worth making a bid to take over another business, Camden and Rush Ltd. There were strong arguments on both sides.

"We've just gone through a period of major expansion," declared Ferdinand Jones, peering over his spectacles at the other board members. "We need now to spend a bit of time consolidating before we consider taking on another risky venture."

Ferdinand was an Oxbridge scholar and might be considered to be the intellectual member of the group. He had a double first in chemistry and had already had a successful career, both in research and management, at a number of big firms working in pharmaceuticals and in the chemical industry. Ferdinand attended board meetings in a tweed jacket, brown corduroy trousers, striped shirt and a tie which didn't really go with the rest of his attire. By contrast, all the other board members wore dark suits which had probably been bought off the peg from Moss Bros if not made to measure. They wore plain white or light blue shirts and conventional ties which coordinated well with the rest of their attire. The only exception was the chairman, Sir Tobias Trelawny, who wore a large spotted bow tie as an accessory to his smartly tailored suit. Sir Tobias was known to favour the arguments presented by Ferdinand.

The next person to speak was Lancelot Ripon. He was the board's finance man, having had a successful career in accountancy in both the private and public sectors.

"I think a takeover bid would be well worth going for. Our accountants have examined Camden and Rush's balance sheets and they think that the firm is in good shape. The price of its shares is low which could mean it's undervalued on the stock market. I think we could acquire Camden and Rush's at a good price."

Terence (Terry) Rastrick spoke next. Terry had joined Chemical Solutions Ltd. when he left school at eighteen and had risen through the firm by hard work. He'd been very popular among the workforce and was a natural to be elected to one of the seats on the board, reserved for workers within the firm who had impressed by their hard work and ability.

"I'm with Ferdinand on this. When considering taking over another firm, it's advisable to look for some overlap where savings can be made by merging these sections. There's no overlap with Henley's. They're supplying a completely different market. No, count me out on this."

Clive Mountjoy wasn't happy with the way the discussion was going.

"Nothing ventured, nothing gained," he almost bellowed from the far end of the table. "Taking over Camden and Rush's will give us a fantastic opportunity to diversify. We've not brought out any new products recently and I think the firm is beginning to get stuck in a rut."

Clive was a sharp faced individual whom people did not immediately take to. He held non-executive directorships on a number of boards. There was no doubt he was shrewd and knew his way around the corporate world and he was also prepared to become ruthless to get things going his way.

The discussion continued for some time and was becoming increasingly heated. Tobias had to step in more than once to prevent tempers from getting out of hand. At last the time came to put the motion to a vote. The result was split fifty-fifty. Lancelot, Clive, Henry and Fergus being in favour of going for the takeover while Ferdinand, Terry, Colin and Christopher were against the idea. Tobias had carefully weighed up the arguments during the discussion and used his casting vote to reject the idea of a takeover. Most of the board stayed for coffee after the meeting but Clive had to dash off to another meeting and Fergus had other business to attend to. Clive and Fergus seldom stayed to socialise at the end of board meetings.

A board meeting held three months later was a much more tranquil affair. There was nothing terribly controversial on the agenda and the business proceeded fairly quickly. This time, only Henry, Ferdinand, Colin and Christopher were able to stay and join Sir Tobias for coffee after the meeting. Julie English, the maid who served the board on these occasions, came in with a tray of cups and a cafetière. Julie was dressed in black, a short skirt, white apron and a lacey white cap. She set out the cups which the members preferred to fill themselves from the cafetière. She offered the sugar from a silver sugar bowl to Sir Tobias who used the tongs to lift two cubes into his cup and sat down as he stirred in the sugar.

Suddenly, Tobias gave a sharp yell, clutched his throat, convulsed and fell off his chair, spilling most of the contents of his cup. Julie screamed. Ferdinand rushed round to Sir Tobias who lay collapsed on the floor. He wasn't breathing. Ferdinand felt both the wrist and then the neck for a pulse. Nothing. Heart massaging didn't work. No defibrillator was available. Sir Tobias was dead.

The police and ambulance were called. The first constable on the scene took notes from those present who seemed to be in a very shattered state. The Scene of Crime Officers took photographs, put the sugar bowl and remaining lumps in a plastic bag and retrieved the coffee cup together with what was left of its contents to go to the pathology lab for examination. The body was placed in a body bag and taken on a stretcher to the ambulance which transferred the body to the police mortuary.

Three days later the board reconvened. Colonel Colin Temporley was unanimously elected chairman to replace Sir Tobias. The matter of taking over Camden and Rush again came up. This time, the vote went in favour of making a hostile takeover bid by four votes to three. Colin, who'd voted against the motion before, was now in the chair and in the absence of a split decision, no casting vote was called for.

<u>**The Investigation**</u>

This case was very different from the ones Peter and Chris had dealt with recently. As usual, their first port of call was the pathology laboratory adjoining the police mortuary where Dr Edward Cooper was on hand to give his assessment of what had happened after the board meeting.

"No dispute this time about the time of death," he claimed. "The victim was poisoned by ingesting potassium cyanide, a very fast acting poison. He would have died almost as soon as he had swallowed the first sip of coffee. Analysis of the remnant of coffee which was retrieved indicates a lethal concentration of the chemical. 200 to 300 milligrams would be sufficient to kill someone and the concentration of cyanide in the coffee would mean that this threshold would have been exceeded by swallowing even a small amount of the stuff. It was probably introduced in the sugar lump which was added to the coffee but the strange thing is that all the sugar lumps left in the bowl were clean, no trace of cyanide at all. Your investigation will hinge on discovering how the contaminated sugar got into the cup. Was it put there by the coffee maid or one of the board members?"

Peter and Chris made their way to the headquarters of Chemical Solutions Ltd. where they had arranged to interview those present when Sir Tobias was fatally poisoned. Lancelot, Clive, Terry and Fergus hadn't been present so there seemed no point in interviewing them at this stage of the enquiry.

Julie English, the maid who had brought the coffee in was the first person they called in. She was much more composed now than she had been at the time of the tragedy but she was clearly very nervous about being interviewed by the police, investigating a murder in which she might be seen to have had some part in what happened. It had been decided that Chris would lead the questioning of this witness.

Chris started, "Miss English, can you describe exactly what happened from the time you were requested to bring in the coffee."

"I brought the coffee in on a large tray," started Julie. "The tray was large because as well as the cups which were stacked, there was a large cafetière, a jug of warm milk, a small jug of cream and a bowl of sugar. I set the cups out. Most of the board members prefer to pour their own coffee. Some like it black, but others may prefer cream or milk and they don't all take sugar, indeed, Sir Tobias is the only member who does take sugar. He usually adds two lumps and stirs it in after he has added the milk."

"So the cups were all empty before the members poured their coffee. Did they have any particular cups which each member regarded as his?"

"Oh no, all the cups are identical."

"Could anyone beside Sir Tobias have put sugar into his cup?"

"No, Sir Tobias served himself last. There were several cups left for him to choose from because I always put out nine cups, not knowing how many members are going to stay on for coffee. After he had poured his coffee, I offered him the sugar bowl and he used the tongs himself to take the usual two lumps."

"Would it be possible for anyone to put a lump of sugar in the bowl before coffee was served at the end of the meeting?"

"Well, yes. There's no secret where the coffee cups, jugs and sugar bowls are kept. It's in a cupboard which isn't locked. The sugar lasts quite a long time because only Sir Tobias takes sugar but I replenish the bowl every couple of months or so. Extra lumps could have been put in the bowl by any person at any time."

"Thank you, Miss English. You've given us a very clear account of how the coffee was served. We're a long way from knowing how the coffee was poisoned but from what you have said, we have a pretty good picture of how the members take their coffee."

Peter and Chris interviewed in turn each of the other board members and they all exactly confirmed the maid's account. They were all some way away from the coffee tray when Sir Tobias poured his own but would have observed in that small gathering, anyone introducing something into Sir Tobias's cup. None of them could suggest anyone who might have had a particular motive to murder Sir Tobias.

At the end of these interviews, Pete deduced that they were now down to four likely suspects.

"You mean the four members who remained to have coffee with Sir Tobias," Chris suggested.

"No, the four board members who hadn't been present on that fateful day."

"However have you reached that conclusion?" asked Chris.

"From the way all five of those interviewed have described the way coffee was served, it's inconceivable that any of them could have put a poisoned lump of sugar into Sir Tobias's cup without it being obvious to everyone else present As Sir Tobias is the only board member who takes sugar in his coffee, whoever wanted to bump him off would only have to leave one lump of poisoned sugar in the bowl," Peter explained. "Although several board meetings may have taken place without Sir Tobias taking the poisoned lump of sugar, at some point after a board meeting, Sir Tobias would have taken the particular lump of sugar from the bowl which killed him. He did that yesterday. This explains why all the remaining sugar lumps were not contaminated with poison. The murderer will assume that we will only suspect someone of poisoning the coffee who was actually drinking coffee with Sir Tobias after the meeting."

"So, we need to look for a board member who made a point of not joining the others after board meetings," responded Chris.

"Exactly. At meetings held at this level where important decisions are made, there is invariably a clerk to take minutes," replied Peter. "I think our next interview must be with the minutes clerk. I think he may well be able to tell us much more than which board member made a point of skipping coffee."

They located the clerk to the directors, a Mr Geoffery Monroe.

Geoffery came to the room where the interviews were being held. Geoffery was a short middle-aged man, dressed in a suit and tie which was very similar to that worn by most of the board members. He brought with him the book which contained the board meeting minutes. No, he never stayed behind for coffee himself. Not every board member stayed for coffee but the only board member he knew who always left with him at the end of the meeting was Mr Mountjoy.

Peter asked Geoffery if there had recently been any particular disagreement on a major policy decision which could have been reversed as a result of Sir Tobias no longer being there. Geoffery paused and thought.

"Yes, there was. Can you wait a few minutes while I go through this file to enable me to give you precise details?"

Geoffery started to leaf through the minutes of meetings held over the past six months. Peter and Chris patiently waited for the best part of quarter of an hour.

"Yes, I've found the details," exclaimed Geoffery with a note of triumph in his voice. "A move was made to launch a takeover bid for Camden and Rush Ltd. The board was split, fifty-fifty so Sir

Tobias used his casting vote to oppose this move. After Sir Tobias died, Colonel Temporley was elected to the chair to replace him. Colonel Temporley was against the takeover but when the matter came up for discussion again, it was carried by four votes to three. Being in the chair, Colonel Temporley couldn't vote as no casting vote was needed."

"What was Mr. Mountjoy's position on this issue?" asked Peter.

"Mr. Mountjoy was in favour of taking over Camden and Rush Ltd."

After they left Chemical Solutions, Peter confided to Chris that he considered that Clive Mountjoy was their prime suspect.

"You may be right," replied Chris, "but we haven't got very much to go on yet. What makes you so sure?"

"I know it's no more than a hunch at this stage. Call it 'policeman's intuition' if you like. The need to get the takeover bid for taking over Camden and Rush could have been so important to someone at that meeting that it had become necessary to kill Sir Tobias. When a thing like that happens in business, it probably means big money is at stake. To uncover any information relevant to this, I'll have to contact Chief Inspector Henry Longstaff of the Financial Fraud Team."

Two days later, Peter had a phone call from the Chief Inspector.

"My word, Peter, you're busy these days with big fraud cases," came Henry's voice. "We do work in the background to investigate the movement of shares when a big takeover is in the offing. We have to check that there's no insider share dealing, that is, someone who has privileged knowledge that there is going to be a takeover uses this information, ahead of it becoming public knowledge, to make a fortune for themselves. In this case, we don't have any direct evidence of insider trading. A certain Penelope Halfpenny has been buying shares in Camden and Rush Ltd. over the past twelve months or so when their price was low and had created a 40% shareholding for herself. She sold the lot soon after the takeover bid was announced and the share value rocketed.

Miss Halfpenny has probably made nearly a million by selling these shares. So far, we haven't been able to trace any direct link between Miss Halfpenny and the board of Chemical Solutions Ltd."

The chief inspector continued,

"Most of the directors of Chemical Solutions have a finger in the pie of other concerns, mostly in the roles of non-executive directors. However, none of them has any direct dealings with Camden and Rush."

He then listed companies in which the directors of Chemical Solutions held interests. Peter was particularly interested in the firms in which Clive Mountjoy held a directorship. 'Henley Pharmaceuticals Ltd.' was a concern which specially arrested Peter's attention.

Peter came away from this phone call, sensing he was on the edge of a breakthrough. He reported to Chris the information he had received from Henry Longstaff and told her that he was going to contact the register of births, deaths and marriages to investigate the background of Miss

Penelope Halfpenny. The registry of births, deaths and marriages used to be located at Somerset House off the Strand but in 1970 was moved to St. Catherine's House in the Aldwych, the other side of the Strand. Peter struck gold. Miss Halfpenny was the maiden name of Mrs. Mountjoy. Penelope was married to Clive Mountjoy. Peter immediately phoned this news back to Henry Longstaff but asked him to delay taking action to expose the insider trading as this might jeopardise his continuing investigation into the murder of Sir Tobias Trelawny.

Chris laughed at the name of the lady who had made a fortune by selling her Camden and Rush shares at the right moment.

"Parents should be more responsible in giving names to their children," she commented. "Poor girl. She must have got fed up with being called Penny Halfpenny at school."

"She was probably very thankful that her parent's surname wasn't 'Farthing'," suggested Peter, "otherwise she might have had to bear being called, 'Old Bike'"

"Anyway, we're there then, aren't we?" asked Chris. "Can we go ahead and make an arrest?"

"We certainly have a case of insider dealing and the Financial Fraud Section will deal with this in due course. We need a bit more evidence before arresting Mr. Mountjoy on a murder charge to ensure the charge will stick. A person with the financial resources of Clive Mountjoy could hire the services of a really clever lawyer who could probably get him off if we go to court, armed only with the evidence we have so far. I've asked DCI Henry Longstaff to hold fire with the fraud investigation until I've done a bit more to investigate the murder. It would be very useful if we could discover how the sugar cube, which was the likely source of poison in Sir Tobias's coffee, could be obtained. I think that I've got a lead. Let's pay a visit to Henley Pharmaceuticals Ltd. where Clive Mountjoy holds a directorship."

Henley Pharmaceuticals Ltd. was a smart factory in a new industrial estate on the edge of town. When Peter and Chris arrived there, the receptionist phoned through to the manager, Mr Edward Jones, to inform him that the police wished to make some enquiries. This was obviously of great concern to the manager who was totally unaware that anything could be going on at Henley's which would require investigation by the police. Instead of getting his secretary to meet them and conduct them to where he was working, he immediately came out of his office and scurried down to the reception desk where he cordially welcomed the detectives and invited them to join him in his office. They accepted his offer of a cup of coffee but they declined the sugar he proffered to them in a bowl.

Mr. Jones was neatly dressed in a Next suit which was showing signs of wear. He wore a white shirt and a bright tie which strangely seemed to go very well with his rather drab suit.

"What can I help you gentlemen with?" - he immediately corrected himself. " --- lady and gentleman with?"

Peter replied.

"We're trying to trace the source of some unusual sugar lumps. Yours seems the sort of business which might be involved in making these."

"Only if they have some medical application. I'm unaware of any such thing being made at Henley's but the person who might know is our chief chemist. Let me take you to his laboratory-cum-workshop and introduce you."

They ascended two storeys in a lift and walked down a long corridor flanked by chambers where staff seemed very busy in their work. They could see through the glass partitions conveyor belts transporting small bottles to be filled, and a machine which appeared to be stamping out rows of tablets. A sheet of some material was being fed into the stamping area at a rate which kept pace with the continuous stamping machine. In another area, liquids were boiling away in stills. At the end of the corridor they entered a half open door into what must have been what Mr Jones had described as a laboratory-cum-workshop. A stout gentleman in a white lab coat was at a workbench. He seemed to be weighing out and mixing powders.

Mr Jones introduced Inspector Sinclair and Sergeant Powers to Dr Stephen Johnson, chief chemist at Henley's. Stephen wore thick horn-rimmed glasses. He had what might be described as a ruddy complexion. Peter and Chris couldn't decide whether that was result of sitting in the sun too long or working at high pressure.

"These police officers are trying to identify the source of what they describe as unusual sugar lumps," explained Mr Jones. "Are you working on anything like that?"

"I just think I might have been."

Dr Johnson made his way to his cluttered desk and gestured to them to sit in the three chairs opposite his rather large swivelling chair of the sort you often find at computer workstations.

"One of our directors," he paused to recollect who it had been, "Yes, of course. it was Mr. Mountjoy. He said he had a contact who was investigating ways of putting down elderly horses which had ended their working life. He wondered if I could make some sugar cubes laced with cyanide. Well, I didn't particularly like the idea. I don't think cyanide poisoning would be a painless death, even for a horse, but we are paid to do our employer's bidding. I made some cubes but fortunately they weren't needed. Mr. Mountjoy's contact had discovered a better way to carry out this task. He asked me to dispose of these cubes."

"Do you still have any of these sugar cubes?" asked Chris, anticipating Peter's next question.

"Actually, I do. I haven't yet worked out the best way of disposing of them. You can't just wash that sort of thing down the sink."

"May we see them?" requested Peter.

Dr Johnson took a set of keys out of a drawer in his desk and led them to a cupboard with a steel door bearing a skull and crossbones sticker on the front. He opened the cupboard. It was full of carefully labelled bottles of tablets.

"Most of the tablets we make could be described as poisonous but only if taken by the wrong people with the wrong dose. Digitalis based medicines are a case in point. That is why you can only get most of them on prescription. They are not freely available over the counter."

He withdrew from the cupboard a glass bottle containing what were obviously sugar cubes.

"Now these are a totally different kettle of fish. I haven't let any go. There's enough cyanide in each of these to kill a horse so they'd certainly be fatal if consumed by a human."

"Has Mr Mountjoy seen them?" asked Chris.

"Oh, yes. This was his project."

"Did he handle them or take any?" she continued.

"Yes, he was very interested in them but I don't think he took any. I would be very concerned if he did. They're highly dangerous."

Peter asked Dr Johnson if he could take the bottle of cubes as they were needed for a police investigation.

Dr Johnson was hesitant.

"Well, yes, in view of the fact that they are needed by the police for what I am sure is an important investigation but you'll have to sign for them before you leave."

Chris thanked Mr Jones and Dr Johnson for the time they'd spent with them. They'd been most helpful. They closed the interview by stressing that they shouldn't let anyone, including the directors, know the purpose of their visit. If the news got out that the police had been nosing around this section of the firm, it could jeopardise their enquiry. They also told Mr Jones to instruct the receptionist not to let anyone know the police had been there. They had reported to her on arrival at Henley's but as plain clothes officers, she would be the only other person to know that police had been in the building.

They left the building in a state of considerable satisfaction.

"I believe we have enough evidence now to proceed with arresting Mr. Mountjoy on a charge, not just of insider trading, but murder," said Peter with a note of triumph in his voice.

The Evidence

The state of the sugar cubes

The fact that the cubes remaining in the bowl were uncontaminated indicated that Sir Tobias, the only board member who took sugar in his coffee, had been killed by a single poisoned cube. The murderer had thought that this would lead the police to believe that one of those taking coffee with Sir Tobias had placed it in his cup. However, the witness statements from all those present indicated that to do this unnoticed in that gathering would have been impossible. Peter deduced that the poisoned sugar cube was already in the bowl, waiting for Sir Tobias to pick this particular cube at some unpredictable date at an after meeting coffee session. Peter independently worked out the murderer's false reasoning and hence deduced that the sugar cube would have been left in the bowl, not by someone at the meeting, but by a person who did not stay for coffee after the meeting. This enabled him to focus on Clive Mountjoy, the only board member who had never stayed behind for the coffee session.

The effect of Sir Tobias's elimination on decisions made by the board.

The clerk to the board, Geoffery Monroe, revealed that the decision not to make a takeover bid for Camden and Rush was reversed when Sir Tobias was no longer around to block the bid. The need to get this decision made could be a motive for murder but who would have benefitted sufficiently make the extreme action of committing a murder worthwhile?

Shareholder who was able to make a fortune as a result of the takeover bid.

Peter recruited the expertise of the Financial Fraud Team to identify who had benefitted from the takeover. The Financial Fraud team are always on the alert for insider trading when takeover bids are afoot. However, at the time CDI Henry Longstaff identified Penelope Halfpenny as an individual who had made a fortune by selling her shares, there was no obvious link with anyone at Chemical Solutions to indicate that insider trading had taken place. By following his hunch and going to the registry of births, deaths and marriages, the fact that Penelope Halfpenny and Clive Mountjoy were married to each other was uncovered. This immediately provided a clear motive for Clive to commit murder.

Source of the poisoned sugar cube

Peter's tenacity in scrutinising Clive Mountjoy's involvement in firms outside Chemical Solutions led him to discover a firm, of which Mr. Mountjoy was director, who could well have prepared the poisoned sugar cube. His visit to Henley Pharmaceuticals revealed that this was exactly where the sugar cube had been made at Clive Mountjoy's request, providing final damning evidence of Clive Mountjoy's guilt.

Chapter 6

Kentisbury Town Band

Victim – Lancelot Henderson - Lead trombonist

Dave Stephens   - Leader and Conductor of
                                    Kentisbury Town Band
Maud Blake   - Secretary to the Band
Edward (Ted) Saundersfoot - Cornet player
Luke Destry   – Saxophonist
John Baker   - Drummer

Colin Avery   – suspected blackmail victim

The Event

The players of Kentisbury Town Band enjoyed playing together. For most members, rehearsals were the social highlight of the week. Lancelot Henderson was the lead trombonist. He was a competent musician. He seemed to get on moderately well with most of his fellow bandsmen but he wasn't popular with everybody. This was because he had a critical nature. He was critical of the hall where the band went to practice, the band's administration, the venues selected when the band played outside Kentisbury and also, the competence, both of other players in the band and of Dave Stephens, the band's leader and conductor. He didn't voice his criticism openly but behind the backs of those against whom his words were targeted.

The event occurred one Sunday afternoon when the band was performing in Campburn Park, one of the main amenities of Kentisbury. The concert had gone well. Lancelot had performed one of the three solos that day and this had been warmly applauded by an audience which had generally enjoyed the band's performance that afternoon.

As the bandsmen were packing away their kit, Lancelot leant forward from his chair, took hold of his music stand, gave a sharp yell and collapsed on the floor. It took a second or too for the other band members to assess what was happening, Then John Baker, who had first-aid experience and usually had more presence of mind than his colleagues, rushed from the timpani section to where Lancelot lay flat of the floor and tested the body for breathing – he wasn't breathing, and pulse – there was no pulse. He stretched out Lancelot's body on the floor, having to release

Lancelot's grip on the music stand as he did this, and attempted mouth to mouth resuscitation and when this didn't work, he tried heart massage, but all to no avail. Lancelot was dead.

The ambulance and police had been contacted by this time and arrived within minutes of each other. The police took statements from some of the bandsmen. The ambulance crew was no more successful than John in resuscitating Lancelot. The two police constables who were first on the scene realised that the death looked suspicious and phoned for backup. In no time, Scene of Crime Officers arrived, took photographs and carefully looked around for anything which might explain this sudden death. Was it just a heart attack? They noticed a burn on the hand which had grasped the music stand. The fact that the music stand was still held tightly in Lancelot's hand as he collapsed suggested he had been killed by an electric shock. This suspicion was supported by the fact that under Lancelot's metal chair was a smallish cardboard box from which protruded two wires. The insulation had been stripped from the ends of each wire and one wire was clamped to the metal base of the chair using a jubilee clip and the other, similarly clamped to the music stand. The wires were hardly noticeable, especially as the wire from the box and connected to the music stand passed under a mat placed in front of Lancelot's chair.

What was in this box? One of the SOCOs opened it to reveal layers of tin foil and polythene and some electronic items wired on to a small motherboard. This didn't mean much to the SOCO and he put it in a bag to be examined more carefully at the forensic laboratory, together with Lancelot's chair and his music stand.

The body was taken to the police mortuary. The band members, who were in a state of shock and had been talking among themselves in subdued tones, dispersed and went home.

Peter and Chris started the investigation by making their usual call to the forensic laboratory where Dr Edward Cooper was expecting them.

"No doubt about cause and time of death," he stated. "The victim was killed by a massive electric shock as he packed away at the end of the concert."

He led them over to a work bench.

"The shock was administered from the contents of this box."

Peter and Chris looked at the box which Edward opened to reveal sheets of tin foil sandwiched between sheets of polythene. The tin foil was connected to electrical components mounted on to a small plastic board and two wires led from the tin foil to separate holes in the box.

Edward continued, "I had a fairly good idea what this was, but I had to consult an electronic engineer to explain exactly what we had here. The tin foil and plastic sheet constitute an electrical capacitor (sometimes, these are called condensers) capable of storing a large electric charge at a high voltage. The electrical components are wired to form what is known as a Cockcroft Walton Voltage Multiplier. This was invented by two physicists, John Cockcroft and Ernest Walton who needed an easy way to generate high voltages, that is of the order of a few kilovolts, to further their experiments in atomic physics. X-ray machines and many television sets will have something like this in their circuitry. Usually, the device is fed with a relatively low voltage output from an alternating current generator which is transmitted via a series of diodes and capacitors connected in series. These accumulate the modest input voltage stored on each capacitor into a very high value. In this case, the ac generator has been replaced by a battery whose output is electronically alternated as it is fed to the bank of capacitors. The final charge generated in the device which killed the victim was stored on the large capacitor made of tin foil and polythene. The circuitry of the system used on Sunday included some switches which could be remotely operated, rather like a car door lock or a television program changer. Thus, the voltage multiplier can be started and stopped externally, the output to the connecting wires switched on remotely and once charged, the capacitor can be remotely discharged. Whoever put this together must regard himself as some sort of electronic whizz kid. I would have expected him to have been able to find a suitable compact commercially available capacitor to do the job instead of making up his own polythene and tin foil job but perhaps he couldn't find one which would reliably work at the sort of voltage required."

Peter summarised what he considered must have happened.

"The cardboard box was installed under Lancelot's chair before the concert. As the concert ended, the murderer would have remotely initiated the device and connected the capacitor to the output as soon as he saw Lancelot start to put his equipment away. Having electrocuted Lancelot, he would have turned off the voltage multiplier and shorted out the capacitor to prevent the wrong person getting a shock."

"Exactly," agreed Edward.

Chris had an important question to ask.

"If the Cockcroft Walton Voltage Multiplier can generate a high voltage in isolation from this tin foil and polythene capacitor, why is the capacitor needed?"

"Good question," replied Edward. "Although the Cockcroft Walton Voltage Multiplier can generate a high voltage output, in order to deliver a lethal shock, the voltage has to be maintained. As soon as any current is drained from the Voltage Multiplier in isolation, the output voltage suddenly drops. By storing the charge on a large capacitor, the voltage will only fall slowly as current is drawn, enabling a lethal shock to be delivered.".

Peter and Chris discussed their approach to solving this case in the light of what Dr Cooper had told them.

"I think it is obvious that our enquiries should initially focus on Kentisbury Town Band," said Peter. "This isn't the first case we've investigated where a member of a music group appears to have been killed by another member of the same group."

"Yes," replied Chris, "but this time we won't be looking for an experienced reptile handler. The method used to despatch the victim is totally different. This time, it looks as if we should be searching out an expert in electronics."

They decided to start their investigation by visiting the band leader, Dave Stephens.

They called at Mr Stephen's house. The door was opened by a smart woman in her mid-forties. This was Mrs Stephens. She was casually dressed in a neat housecoat and stylish carpet slippers. Peter and Chris hardly had to introduce themselves and show their warrant cards.

"We've been expecting the police to call about that bad business on Sunday. It's been a terrible shock to Dave. He always considered that the band was a really happy group with no serious antagonism among any of them."

She showed them into a large living room where Dave Stephens was seated at a piano, trying out variations on tunes. Steve was about the same age as his wife. He was wearing dark jeans and a check shirt with rolled up sleeves. When he stood to meet them, they realised that Dave was exceptionally tall.

"Bad business on Sunday," he said as he met them.

He gestured to a settee and sat opposite them in an armchair. Chris, who was interested in furniture, felt sure that the suite where they were now sitting was Parker-Knoll. It bore a tasteful pattern and the curtains were of a similar but not identical pattern. The furniture was set off well against a plain fawn coloured carpet which looked fairly new. Dave hardly needed prompting to tell them about his feeling for the band and in particular, the victim, Lancelot.

Dave reiterated what his wife had said about the shock he experienced at something as serious as murder being committed among a group he knew well and whom he believed all got on well together.

"Lancelot was perhaps the only one who was in any way a bit of a misfit," explained Dave. "He wasn't entirely popular because he had a tendency to run people down behind their backs. I know that I came in for some criticism from that quarter myself but I have broad shoulders. The boss is always first in the firing line when criticism is afoot. I know that Dave isn't the only member of the band who thinks that I should have done some things differently, but that's all part of the burden of leadership."

Although acknowledging that Lancelot wasn't popular, he couldn't identify anyone who seemed particularly antagonistic towards Lancelot, certainly not to the extent that they would resort to murder.

Peter then started to question on a different tack. He asked Dave if there was anyone in the band who seemed to have a particular interest in electronics.

Dave laughed at this question."

"A significant proportion of the band members work for 'Circuit Solutions Ltd.', one of the main employers in this area. I believe that quite a few of them dabble in electronics as a hobby."

Dave was able to furnish our detectives with a list of names and addresses of everybody associated with the band. Pete and Chris were very grateful for this as they set about planning future interviews.

Peter next asked Dave if anyone could have seen a box being placed under Lancelot's seat.

"When we play in Campburn Park, Joe, Clive and Michael, (they're three of our band members) come down in the morning and set up the band stand. The seats and music stands are all stored under the band stand. With the three of them working together, they usually get the job done in an hour, an hour and a half at the outside."

"Could one of these three have placed the box there?"

"Not without being seen by the others and I understand that they all left together after setting up. I hardly think that the three of them were involved in a conspiracy to murder Lancelot.

However, if someone went to the bandstand after Joe, Clive and Michael left, they could have quite easily installed that lethal device. The bandsmen all sit in the same places every performance so any band member would know exactly where Lancelot would be sitting. The playing area is quite accessible and no-one would take much notice of someone who seemed to be going about normal business in the bandstand. Indeed, I imagine that was just how the device was installed. You may be able to find a witness who observed and could identify the lone person who appeared to be involved in setting up the bandstand sometime that morning but I rather think that's a long shot."

The detectives thanked Dave for the time he'd spent with them.

"That's been helpful but only of limited help," Peter confided to Chris as they left the Stephens' house. "However, Dave has probably described exactly how the lethal box was placed under Lancelot's chair."

"Where do we go from here?" asked Chris.

"I think that it might be worth calling on Maud Blake, the band secretary. She wasn't at the concert so she's hardly a suspect but she might be able to give us a balanced account of the band members, their characteristics, strengths and weaknesses and the relationships which existed between them."

Peter and Chris were unable to interview Maud during the day as she worked full-time as an administrator at Circuit Solutions. This was useful as it might mean Maud could throw light on band members in both their recreational and professional environments. They didn't think it wise to enter her work situation to conduct an interview at this stage of their investigation so they arranged to meet her at her home before her evening meal.

Maud was a tall, very serious looking woman, smartly dressed with short hair. When the detectives called on her, she was still in her work clothes, a navy suit and cream blouse. She wore square framed spectacles. She cordially invited them in.

"I know you've called about what happened to Lancelot," she began. "What a bad business. I didn't like him. I don't think anybody in the band did but no-one in the band would go to the extreme of killing him, just because they didn't like him."

Chris asked the first question.

"Why wasn't he liked and was there anybody who showed particular dislike towards him?"

"Not really. By and large, the band members are very tolerant and they'd always have been courteous to Lancelot, even if they didn't like him. Lancelot's main trouble lay in the fact that he spent a lot of time gossiping about band members behind their backs and was always fishing for any other information about members which was really none of his business."

"What sort of information?"

"Oh, how people got on at work, did they have good or bad marriages, what were their kids like, and that sort of thing."

Peter took up the questioning.

"As you probably know, Lancelot was electrocuted with a remotely controlled device. Is there anyone in the band whom you think might have had the expertise to make such a thing?"

Maud laughed.

"Like myself, a lot of them work for Circuit Solutions and some are quite clever. Most of the band members work on production lines but our cornet player, Ted Saundersfoot, is a chartered electrical engineer and he works on the development of complex components. Our saxophonist, Luke Destry, programmes microchips. I think they're the only ones capable of making the thing that killed Lancelot but on the other hand, they're such decent fellows. I don't think they'd be capable of murder."

Peter and Chris thanked Maud for information which helped them understand the social and professional relationships of band members. As they left Maud's house, Peter told Chris that things related to money sometimes provided the motive for murder. He therefore suggested that it

174

would be a good idea to examine Lancelot's bank account. As the police required this in pursuit of a murder enquiry, they experienced no difficulty in having the bank make this available.

For the most part, the bank statement showed normal deposits and payments, a monthly salary entry, grocery bills, small purchases, utility bills paid by standing order and so on. However, the bank record did indeed have features which suggested a further line of enquiry. Five years earlier, regular monthly payments of £100 started to be paid into Lancelot's account by a person named G. Henderson. Six months after G. Henderson had started making these payments, another set of payments of £100 a month were being paid into Lancelot's account, this time by someone named Colin Avery. A year later, another series of monthly £100 payments appeared, this time from a name they recognised, Edward Saundersfoot. A year later still, all these payments suddenly increased to £150 and they were still being paid, up to the time of Lancelot's death.

"What do you make of this?" Peter asked Chris.

"I think we have uncovered something which could well prove a motive for murder," Chris suggested. "I think these regular payments are being received from individuals who were being blackmailed by Lancelot!"

"That's exactly my thought," agreed Peter. "As one of these individuals is a band member, Ted Saundersfoot has now become a prime suspect for the murder of Lancelot."

"So do we go and interrogate him?"

"Not yet. So far, we've only circumstantial evidence. We're not even sure that the payments he made to Lancelot were blackmail payoffs. We need to gather a bit more evidence. I'll check to make sure that the forensic team have taken a set of fingerprints from the contents of the box which was placed under Lancelot's chair. They should have got some good prints from the foil.

To check out our blackmail theory, we'll contact one of the other names who was paying into Lancelot's account before we confront Ted."

They managed to locate Colin Avery. He wasn't local but lived in a suburb of Birmingham. Colin was not surprisingly a little alarmed when Peter told him that they were police detectives investigating a crime in another part of the country. They assured him that he was in no way suspected of any crime. At the time, Peter and Chris had no idea of what Colin was being blackmailed over, if indeed they were dealing with a case of blackmail, but if Lancelot was blackmailing Colin in connection with an undetected crime which Colin had committed, this would have made him very wary about being interviewed by the police. They arranged to meet Colin by the duck pond in Handsworth Park in Birmingham. Colin gave a description of himself and said he would be carrying a red shopping bag for ease if identification.

They had no problem in locating Colin at the prearranged time and rendezvous. He was undoubtedly a handsome man wearing a stylish suit and coordinating tie which Peter and Chris assumed were his office clothes. Peter came straight to the point.

"We're investigating a case of blackmail. As your name has been noticed as paying regular sums of money into the suspected blackmailer's account, we wondered if you too were a victim."

Colin was forthcoming. Yes, Lancelot had discovered through a contact he had in Birmingham that Colin had had an affair and he threatened to tell Colin's wife unless he made the required payments. The affair was long since over and Colin couldn't imagine how he could have been so stupid as to embark on this clandestine affair. He desperately loved his wife who was the only real love of his life. He was concerned that what he had done would break up his family. He greatly loved his three beautiful children. He was prepared to do anything to avoid their discovering his infidelity. He was easy prey for a blackmailer. Colin almost wept as he recounted this sorry tale.

Peter and Chris told Colin that he had provided very useful confirmation of something they already suspected. They assured him that they certainly wouldn't be contacting his wife. They also passed on to Colin the information that Lancelot was dead. This was no doubt a great source of relief for Colin. They didn't disclose the details of Lancelot's death and clearly, Colin hadn't read about the murder in the newspapers.

As they drove down the M42 away from Birmingham, Chris expressed her confidence that they had now fairly conclusively identified Mr Edward Saundersfoot as the murderer.

"When should we arrange to interview him?" she asked Peter.

"Before doing that," explained Peter, "I think that we should be prepared to get a set of his fingerprints. If these match up with any discovered on the lethal cardboard box and its contents, we'll have conclusive proof of Ted's guilt."

The next day they called at Ted Saunderfoot's address out of working hours when he was expected to be at home. It transpired that he was a bachelor living alone in a small, one bedroom flat. Ted was in shirtsleeves when he opened the door. He was stockily built with a swarthy complexion. He invited them in after they had introduced themselves and shown him their warrant cards. The room was small but very tidy.

It didn't look like the sort of place where Ted might have dabbled in building electronic devices. However, if he was involved in a research capacity at Circuit Solutions, he would have ample opportunity at work in an environment where any component needed to build the device which killed Lancelot would be readily available

"We're making enquiries into the death of Lancelot Henderson who was killed at the end of last Sunday's band concert," started Peter. "We believe he was known to yourself."

"I didn't know him well," answered Ted. "He was a fellow bandsman and we performed together at band events but we didn't really socialise."

"Do you know how he was killed?" asked Peter.

"I gather he received a major electric shock but I've no idea how it could have been delivered."

Peter took out from his briefcase a laminated card bearing a circuit diagram and handed it to Ted.

"Do you recognise this circuit?"

Ted stiffened as he received the card. They sensed that now, Ted realised he must be very much on guard over what he said. It was obvious that he immediately recognised the circuit but paused for quite a while before he answered.

"This looks like a voltage multiplier but it couldn't have been used to kill poor Lancelot. First, even when it had built up a significant voltage, it wouldn't deliver enough power to be lethal, and in any case, the circuit shows that this sort of voltage multiplier has to be fed from a transformer which would normally be fed from the mains. There's no mains socket on the floor of the bandstand."

Chris now took up the questioning. She had an A level in physics.

"But isn't it true that one could arrange for a circuit to be switched on remotely which could alternate the output from an ordinary battery to the voltage multiplier?"

Ted paused again before answering this question.

"Yes, but a chip would need to be programmed to provide such an alternating device. Somebody at Circuit Solutions who specialises in programming microchips might be able to do this but offhand, I can't think who."

"Yes," continued Chris with her interrogation, "but a microchip is only a very compact equivalent of a circuit made with conventional electronic components. I think it's called SSI, small scale integration. Couldn't the voltage multiplier be fed from a circuit which used conventional electronic components rather than a microchip?"

Chris knew very well that this was exactly how the circuit had been set up and realised that Ted was bluffing in his apparent ignorance of this possibility.

"Yes, now you mention this, that would certainly be possible."

Ted was thinking to himself, "Who are these hitech cops. I didn't think the police had training in this sort of thing."

Peter then took up the questioning.

"We believe that you were being blackmailed by Lancelot. Had he recently hiked up his demands?"

Ted suddenly looked drawn. He realised that the police must have scrutinised Lancelot's bank accounts.

"The fact that I've been paying money to Lancelot doesn't mean he was blackmailing me and it's none of your business anyway."

"Everything's our business when we're pursuing a murder inquiry and you almost certainly must know that Lancelot was murdered. You weren't the only person being blackmailed by Lancelot. We've interviewed someone whose pattern of payments into Lancelot's account was exactly the same as yours and he's told us that he was being blackmailed. Are you able to tell us anything more about the payments you made to Lancelot?"

"No further comment," Ted replied blandly.

"Very well," concluded Peter. "We'll leave you now but we'll be calling on you again tomorrow when perhaps you'll feel like furnishing us with more information about why you made these payments into Lancelot's account over such an extended period."

Peter slipped the laminated circuit diagram back into his brief case and stood to leave. Ted showed them out.

As expected, Ted's fingerprints on the laminated circuit diagram matched those found on the tinfoil in the lethal box which had been used to kill Lancelot. The following day, two uniformed officers called on Edward Saundersfoot and after declaring the standard words of caution, arrested him on the charge of murdering Lancelot Henderson.

The Evidence.

The location of the box containing the device used to kill Lancelot

The fact that all the bandsmen knew where each would be sitting and that the box was placed under and connected to the very chair that was going to be used by Lancelot, indicated that the murder had been carried out by a member of the band.

The nature of the device used to kill Lancelot

The fact that some technical knowledge was needed to construct such a device immediately narrowed the search. The police would be looking for someone with the required technical knowhow. The likely suspects would be bandsmen who were also employees of Circuit Solutions.

Lancelot's bank statements

The detectives spotted a pattern of payments into the bank which suggested that Lancelot was involved in blackmail. This suspicion was confirmed by one of the victims of Lancelot's blackmail. This discovery also meant that a strong motive for murder had been uncovered.

Ted Saundersfoot's name appearing against the regular payments to Lancelot's account.
This narrowed the search down to one prime suspect who satisfied the other conditions of being a member of the band and someone with the necessary technical knowledge to construct the lethal electronic device. Ted never disclosed what Lancelot knew which enabled him to blackmail Ted.

Fingerprint evidence
The fingerprints that Peter obtained on the laminated circuit sheet provided the final conclusive evidence that Ted Saundersfoot was the murderer, as the prints matched those found on material in the box which contained the lethal electronic device.

Chapter 7

<u>Staged Murder</u>

Victim - Josiah Cunningham – cast
         member playing Lord Stuart
               Cavendish

Westmorland Players
Marcus Hamilton – Producer
Hilary Barton - Administrator

Actors and Actresses
Helen Winslow – playing Mary
               Throckmorton
Peter Thornton
Gordon Edwards
Joan Stephens
James Fourier

Stagehands and Technicians
Jack Milton
Alex Carpenter
Philip Jones

Joe Adamson – manager of 'Rifleman',
        the gun shop in Birmingham

The Event

The Westmorland Players were now performing at the Majestic in Framlington. Their latest production, 'Hell hath no Fury' was one of their most successful ever. It had played to packed audiences as it toured the country and tonight would be the final performance at the Majestic before the company packed up and moved on to a new venue. Those who had an inside knowledge of the players and the relationship between them might have considered the title of this particular play a bit ironic. 'Hell hath no fury like a woman scorned' might have described the underlying tensions which existed between some of the actors in this troop.

Two of the actors, Peter Thornton and James Fourier were discussing a third member of the troop, Josiah Cunningham, whom they evidently disliked. Josiah was an extremely handsome man in his early thirties. Not only was he handsome but he was a brilliant actor. However, these attributes were counterbalanced by some negative character traits. He was vain, selfish and immoral. Josiah had a history of seducing girls in previous towns where the company had performed.

A particular scandal was associated with their visit to a large industrial town a few years earlier. A young woman called Sarah Jones and her unborn baby had died as a result of a botched back-street abortion. Josiah was suspected of being the father but nothing was proved and Sarah's family shunned any publicity associated with this tragedy. In spite of his reputation, some of the female members of the troop still became infatuated with Josiah and were embroiled in short term romances before Josiah turned his attention elsewhere.

"Many times, I've thought of leaving Westmorland Players to join another company, just to get away from Josiah," Peter confided to James, "but as you know, acting is a precarious profession. Westmorland Players is such a successful company and pays well so that it's difficult to secure a comparable situation in another troop."

"I can sympathise with your sentiments," James responded. "The thing that I most dislike about Josiah is not his vanity, deplorable though that is, but the way he treats women, specially fellow company members."

Because they recognised the base sort of person that Josiah was, neither Peter nor James felt envious of Josiah for his looks and talent. Peter did however feel envious of the fact that the beautiful Helen Winslow had fallen for Josiah's superficial charm. James felt sympathy for Gordon Edwards, another member of the troop, who had formerly been regarded as making up an item with Helen. In contrast to Josiah, Gordon was a very popular member of the troop.

"I've every hope that Helen will soon return to Gordon," suggested James. "I believe that Helen and Josiah have had a bit of a falling out recently."

"Well, that's good news and not really surprising," said Peter, "because Josiah has started to pay a bit too much attention to Joan."

Joan Stephens was another member of the company who had thus far managed to keep Josiah at arm's length.

Peter and James continued to share memories of deplorable episodes in Josiah's romantic history and the tragic death of Sarah Jones came up. Peter and James were convinced that Josiah had been the lover of Sarah and father of her unborn child.

The theatre was packed for the final performance of 'Hell hath no Fury'. The final act was drawing to a close. Mary Throckmorton (played by Helen Winslow) strode on to the stage to confront Lord Stuart Cavendish (played by Josiah Cunningham).

"If you think you are going to get away with the despicable way you have behaved," Mary fairly bellowed at Lord Stuart, "you've got another thing coming."

With that, Mary withdrew a pistol from the bag she was carrying and fired it at Lord Stuart at point blank range. Lord Stuart fell heavily, more heavily than usual. The curtain came down marking that the play had concluded with this dramatic event.

On every previous night, the curtain had only remained down for a few seconds. This allowed the cast to gather on stage before the curtain was raised again. Then the cast bowed in response to the tumultuous applause which expressed the appreciation of the audience of this wonderful production. However, tonight was different. Lord Stuart did not get to his feet. There was a blood stain on the front of his tunic. Marcus Hamilton, the producer rushed on to the stage to check out what had happened to Lord Stuart (Josiah Cunningham). He discovered that Josiah wasn't breathing. He had no pulse. Josiah was dead. This fact was announced by a shocked Marcus as he stood up from the body. Mary Throckmorton (Helen Winslow) fainted.

Marcus went in front of the curtain to announce that it wouldn't be raised as an accident had occurred on the stage. The audience murmured in puzzlement as they left the theatre and dispersed. The police and ambulance were contacted. Statements were taken, the body photographed, the gun was put in a plastic bag to be examined by forensics and finally, the body of Josiah Cunningham was removed to the police mortuary.

The company were told to delay their move to the town where their next performance was due to open in a fortnight's time until the police had finished their enquiries regarding this untimely death. They all had comfortable accommodation in local hotels and there was no problem in arranging for their stays to be extended.

The Investigation

Peter and Chris attended the forensic laboratory, their usual first port of call before commencing an investigation, to ascertain whether the pathologist, Dr Edward Cooper, had come up with anything which might suggest leads.

"Death was the result of a single bullet fired into the heart," declared Edward. "The gun recovered from the set was the murder weapon. From what I've heard of the circumstances in which this poor fellow was killed, I rather think the culprit was the person who loaded the gun rather than the actress who fired it. Otherwise, I've no further information which might help you in your enquiries."

Peter and Chris had already decided that it was unlikely that Helen had loaded the gun. They started their investigation by visiting Marcus Hamilton who had produced the play. Marcus was a chubby, good natured looking man. He was wearing a blue striped shirt under a navy waist coat. He was clearly shaken by what had happened the previous evening.

"Josiah wasn't a particularly nice person," Marcus began as he started to explain to the detectives something about the members of the company. "He was a lady's man who really fancied himself. He formed a number of short-term relationships, both with members of the company and with young women in the towns where the Westmorland Players were performing. Some of these affairs had tragic consequences. I know that Josiah was having a dalliance with Helen and although she'd actually fired the gun, I certainly don't believe that she's a murderer. She's a mature, self-possessed woman who has a great career in acting ahead of her. I've been led to believe that she was in the process of breaking any sort of romantic relationship with Josiah and not that he was ditching her. I can't think why an intelligent woman like Helen should have allowed herself to get into a relationship with Josiah anyway. We all knew what he was like. However, some men seem to be irresistibly attractive to women, whatever their reputation. Sadly, I'm not one of them."

Marcus chuckled as he made this final self-deprecating remark.

Chris resumed the questioning.

"If you don't believe that Helen murdered Josiah, someone else must have loaded the gun. Have you any ideas who this might be?"

Marcus shrugged his shoulders.

"Normally, this would have been done by one of our three stagehands, Jack Milton, Alex Carpenter or Philip Jones, before the performance. However, when under pressure, we all muck in together and the actors help with getting things ready for a performance. Anyone could have loaded the gun."

"Last night, it must have been loaded with a live round," continued Chris in her interrogation. "Do you have live rounds on the set?"

"Certainly not. The live round must have been obtained by whoever was intent on killing Josiah."

"I imagine that normally the gun would have been loaded with a blank cartridge which made a noise but would do no damage. Where do you get these cartridges from?"

"Quite right. Up until yesterday, it's always been 100% safe. As our current play has had a long run covering several venues, we've used up several boxes of blank cartridges. We get them from 'Rifleman', a gun store in Birmingham which accepts our licence to purchase ammunition. When we're going through a slack period, usually between shows when we're moving from one town to another, one of the stagehands goes to Birmingham to pick up a new box. Our supplier doesn't like sending ammunition, even if it's blanks, through the post or even by one of the courier firms which specialises in parcel delivery. However, if one of our actors wants a day out in Birmingham, and this often happens, they collect a fresh cartridge box."

"Do you have a record of which individuals have collected ammunition from this shop?"

"No, but I rather think that our administrator, Hilary Barton will have. She's very efficient and doesn't miss much."

Peter and Chris located Hilary in the lounge of the hotel where she had been billeted. Hilary was a woman of late middle age. Chris assessed her as being in her mid-fifties. She was languishing in a deep armchair, watching the communal television and sipping from what appeared to be a cocktail which she replaced on a mat on the coffee table beside her chair as the detectives entered. There was no-one else present in the lounge. Hilary gathered a black lace shawl round her as she stood to greet the detectives. She guessed who they might be as soon as they entered the room. Hilary was quite forthcoming and started to express her angle on the situation as soon as Peter had announced their business.

"I must say that I'm not entirely surprised at what happened. Some discarded female was bound to have sought to make an end of Josiah at some point, but although she fired the gun, I'm sure Helen hadn't believed it to be loaded with a live round. Helen's for too sensible a woman to commit murder like that because of a lovers' tiff. Helen's lovely. She could have any man she wanted. Why ever she took up with Josiah beats me. He was a nasty bit of stuff."

Chris continued with the interrogation. This was usually her role when a female was being questioned.

"Have you any idea who might have loaded the gun with a live round?"

"It could have been anyone. Josiah was a real shitbag. There must be plenty of people in the company and beyond who would have been glad to see him dead. The downside is that the loss of Josiah could affect our bookings. He was a brilliant actor, a favourite with the ladies who didn't know him personally and quite a box-office draw."

"Mr Hamilton said that you might have records of who would have collected the ammunition you use from a shop in Birmingham."

"The shop's called 'Rifleman'. It's normally one of the stagehands, Jack, Alex or Philip. Sometimes, it's one of the actors. Let me check my records. I'll have to go to my room. When you work with an itinerant group, it isn't just living out of a suitcase. If you're an administrator, you have to live out of a briefcase as well. You'd be surprised at how much paperwork I have to carry around with me."

Hilary left and returned a few minutes later with a bulging briefcase. She sat down and rummaged through it.

"Are, here it is," she said as she withdrew a sheet of paper. "The last one who went to collect ammunition was Jack Milton in June. I don't seem to have a note of who went the time before that. I'll have a look at the invoices we've received from Rifleman."

Hilary rummaged through her briefcase again and came out with a pile of a dozen or so sheets. She looked through them.

"I have the June invoice here. Yes, cartridges were bought in April but I don't know who went to collect them, but here's something interesting. The invoice is a bit different. The main pack of cartridges are listed under one part number and an extra pack of six cartridges is listed under a different number."

She looked back to the June invoice.

"Yes, the cartridges bought in June are listed under the same part number as the main purchase in April."

Hilary looked up from her papers to the detectives.

"Do you think the extra six cartridges bought in April were live rounds?"

"I think that's probably the case," said Peter.

They spent the rest of the day interviewing the other members of the company and came away with their heads buzzing after hearing the long list of Josiah's relationships which had turned sour. Helen, the one who'd fired the gun was particularly distraught, not just because it was her hand that delivered the fatal shot but that she'd been stupid enough to get involved with Josiah in the first place. She'd been well aware that he was a rotter, but even rotters, perhaps specially rotters, can have a magic charm about them. Joan Stephens, the other actress whose name had come up in connection with Josiah, admitted she'd felt a bit flattered when Josiah had started to pay her attention but insisted that she was certainly not romantically involved with him.

While the stagehands were unlikely to have been affected by Josiah's romantic escapades, one of these was likely to have loaded the gun. One of them had probably collected the cartridges from the gun shop. Jack Milton, the senior technician and stagehand, admitted that it would normally have been his job to load the gun. Over the last few months, he had found the gun already loaded on several occasions when he went to check it. This hadn't particularly surprised him as everybody, including the actors, mucked in to get everything ready before curtain up and as everyone knew where the props were kept and how they were organised, anyone could have loaded the gun as one of the jobs known to be necessary before the show began.

When questioned about going to Birmingham to collect the ammunition from 'Rifleman', he remembered picking them up in June. He had to think hard to remember what happened in April. Then it came back to him. Both he and Alex Carpenter, another stage hand, had been given time off over Easter as the company was in a slack period just after finishing a run at the Belgrade in Coventry, He explained that the downside of being part of an itinerant theatre company was that they were away from their families most of the year. Jack had gone to his home in Portsmouth and Alex had returned to London. When they returned from leave, they found the cartridges had already been collected. Alex Carpenter independently confirmed what Jack had told them concerning his own whereabouts during Easter. He had spent time at his home in London.

Peter and Chris now turned their attention to the youngest of the stagehands, Philip Jones. 'No', he hadn't loaded the gun. 'Yes', he had remained with the company during Easter preparing scenery for their next production but 'No', he hadn't been the one who collected the ammunition on that occasion.

At the end of the day, Peter and Chris returned home feeling that they hadn't got very far in positively identifying the one responsible for Josiah's murder. Anyone of them could have done it. Several of them had motives. Peter and Chris felt that they'd no really strong leads. Was it a conspiracy where several of the company had worked together to end Josiah's life? That seemed unlikely. They would all have had to be involved to make that work and not everyone in a group that size, if any, would have been prepared to be involved in murder.

When Peter and Chris met the following morning, Peter told Chris that overnight he'd thought of a new way to follow up their line of enquiry. Something they hadn't already done was to call at 'Rifleman', the gun shop, to see if they could pick up any leads there.

Peter and Chris met Joe Adamson, the manager of Rifleman in his office at the back of the shop. Joe was of average height and build, clean shaven and slightly balding. He had put on his tweed jacket when he knew the police wished to make enquiries. He was clearly anxious when the police showed an interest in what he had been selling.

"We do sell other things besides guns and ammunition," he explained but he insisted, "we only sell guns and ammunition to customers who have the necessary licences. Yes, we do sell blank ammunition to Westmorland Players and indeed to other theatre companies but they all have the necessary licence."

"We are particularly interested in a sale made to Westmorland in April," Peter explained. "Do you have any paperwork associated with this sale?"

"We certainly will have," replied Joe. "In this business, it's vital we keep track of what goes on and maintain good records."

Joe left his office and returned about five minutes later with the required documents. Peter and Chris recognised that this was a copy of the invoice that Hilary Barton had shown them.

After casting his eyes over the document, Peter made an intelligent guess and observed,

"As well as blank ammunition, six rounds had been supplied under a part number which corresponds to live ammunition."

This observation caught Joe Adamson by surprise. How could this policeman know what sort of ammunition was being supplied by a six digit part number? He took back the invoice.

"Yes," he said in an astonished voice. "Westmorland's standing order with us is for blank cartridges. I can't think why there should have been live rounds included in this batch."

"Do you think the person who came to collect these rounds asked for the extra ammunition when he arrived at the counter?"

"Yes, that's possible but our counter assistant shouldn't have supplied live rounds without checking with someone senior to himself."

Joe looked at the invoice again.

"Yes," he said, "the salesperson was a new, inexperienced employee who didn't know the ropes at the time. He left our employment after only six months. I might be able to furnish you with his address but I think he was the sort of person who moves on quickly so he may well be anywhere by now."

"Well, thank you for that," continued Peter. "We'll come back to you if we find we really need to contact this counter assistant to help us identify the person who collected the ammunition but I think that will be unlikely. I imagine the person collecting the ammunition would have signed for it."

"Of course," said Joe. "His signature should be on the copy of the invoice."

He handed the invoice back to Peter.

A rubber stamp had been used to print at the bottom of the invoice,
'RECEIVED 20th April 2015'
The signature next to this was no more than an illegible piece of scribble.

"May I keep this invoice?" asked Peter.

"Yes, of course if the police need it but I'll need to first take a photocopy to ensure my records are intact."

Joe left and returned a few moments later and handed Peter the invoice.

After thanking Joe for his help, Peter and Chris returned the Majestic Theatre which was the temporary headquarters for the Westmorland

Players in Framlington until the next company needed to take up residence.

"You haven't completely filled me in with your plan to continue our enquiries," Chris said to Peter.

"The more I thought about it overnight," Peter explained "I realised there was a connection we'd overlooked and I've a hunch this could be important. A name which came up several times when we interviewed the members of the company was Sarah Jones who'd died during an abortion of what many believed to be Josiah's baby. One of the stagehands is called Jones. It seems that he joined the company not long after the death of Sarah. Jones is such a common surname but there's still a possibility Philip and Sarah are related. I'll be able to find this out by contacting the register of births, deaths and marriages in the Aldwych. Meanwhile, I'll need to obtain from Marcus Hamilton a copy of Philip's signature which I can use if my hunch proves right."

Peter's hunch proved right. Sarah and Philip were brother and sister.

They arranged to interview Philip again.

I understand that your sister, Sarah, died about eighteen months ago in unfortunate circumstances," was Peter's opening gambit.

Philip had an alarmed look as he stared first at Peter and then Chris.

"How did the police know about this?" he thought.

"Yes, it was very sad."

"Do you know who was the father of the unborn baby?"

"No, that never came out."

Peter and Chris sensed that Philip was lying.

"Would it surprise you to know that Josiah Cunningham was the father?" continued Peter.

Philip sat impassively showing no surprise, no other reaction.

"Yes, I would be surprised."

"How does what I've told you make you feel about Josiah Cunningham?"

"I'm glad he's dead," replied Philip without any show of emotion.

This unnatural impassive response confirmed in Peter and Chris's minds that Philip had known all along about the relationship between his sister and Josiah.

"We understand that you went to collect the blank ammunition used in the play in April" said Peter as he continued the interview.

"No," protested Philip "I was preparing scenery right through the first part of April until the opening night in Bristol."

"Well," replied Peter, "How is it that we have a receipt signed by yourself, certifying that you'd received the ammunition from 'Rifleman'?"

Philip looked worried.

"Can I see the receipt? he asked.

"Peter handed Philip what appeared to be the receipted invoice.

"Isn't that your signature?" he asked.

Philip studied the invoice for sometime.

"Yes, it looks like my signature but I didn't sign the receipt at 'Rifleman' like that."

Philip had fallen into the trap.

"Did you sign it like this?" Pater said, producing the genuine receipted invoice with the illegible scribbled signature.

Philip realised the game was up. "Yes, I bought the live cartridges, I put them in the gun and I'm glad that I did. A snake like Josiah doesn't deserve to live. I'm glad it's all come out now. I'm proud of what I did."

Philip Jones was arrested for the murder of Josiah Cunningham. He was told on his arrest that he didn't need to say anything, but anything he did say could be used as evidence at his trial.

<u>**The Evidence**</u>

There was very little evidence in this case to enable the murderer to be conclusively identified and had it not been for Peter's intuition, the case would have taken much longer to solve.

The receipted copy of the invoice
This was perhaps the main tangible piece of concrete evidence. The illegible signature was a clear indication that whoever had collected the ammunition didn't want to be identified. So many people have illegible signatures these days that a signature is no longer a reliable form of identity. However, the trick that Peter played by preparing a false invoice which bore a forged, legible copy of the signature that Philip usually used, was sufficient to catch Philip out in an unguarded moment and led to his admission of guilt.

Discovery of live cartridges
After Philip had been arrested, a search was made of his room. Five live rounds which could have been used with the gun used in the theatre performance were discovered. This discovery was all that was needed to conclusively prove

Philip Jones' guilt and he was successfully prosecuted.

<u>Epilogue</u>

When Peter and Chris discussed the case together later, they recognised what a destructive emotion revenge can be. They contrasted Philip Jones' attitude with that of John Foster whom they'd encountered in a previous case.

"I really took to John," said Peter. "He shares our Christian faith in a very meaningful way. He really did make Jesus the person on whom he decided to model his life."

"Yes," agreed Chris, "He forgave the person who'd brutally murdered his wife and thus, was able to continue life, saddened of course, but at peace with himself. Philip Jones on the other hand had destroyed his chance of living a fruitful productive life by pursuing his need to avenge his sister's death. It's been said that a person who refuses to forgive, burns the bridge which he will need to receive forgiveness in turn himself, and which of us does not need forgiveness?"